"INSPIRATIO

"*Lincoln Park* provides a refreshing and innovative way to nurture the spirituality of young adolescents! The story triggers the curiosity and engages the imagination of young teens as they discover the sacred in surprising and relevant ways. The characters and situations they encounter explore the common questions and concerns, doubts, and dreams that weave life and faith into an adventure of *being* and *believing* for young adolescents. *Lincoln Park* brings the holy to light as young adolescents discover the sacred in ordinary life!"

Mary Lee Becker, *Young Adolescent Ministry Consultant*

"This book is very inspirational in a way that shows how even teenagers can make a difference in their communities. I loved the way I had to search for hidden messages throughout this book. It gave me time to think about the choices they were making. I felt like I could relate to the story because of the up-to-date teenage problems. This was an amazing book that sent meaningful messages about how to prepare for your future and how wisdom is more important than possessions."

Alysa age 14

ABOUT THE AUTHORS

John Shea

John (Jack) Shea is a theologian and storyteller who lectures nationally and internationally on storytelling in world religions, faith-based health care, contemporary spirituality, and the spirit at work movement.

Jack was previously a professor of systematic theology and the Director of the Doctor of Ministry Program at the University of St. Mary of the Lake, a research professor at the Institute of Pastoral Studies at Loyola University of Chicago, and the Advocate Healthcare Senior Scholar in Residence at the Park Ridge Center for the Study of Health, Faith and Ethics. He has also taught at the University of Notre Dame and Boston College.

Jack has published thirteen books of theology and spirituality and two books of poetry.

Mike Carotta

An author and nationally renowned speaker, Dr. Michael Carotta has worked with adolescents and their spiritual growth in educational, pastoral, and clinical settings for more than twenty-five years. A long time catechist, Mike has also served as Diocesan Director of Adolescent Catechesis, Executive Director of the NCEA Department of Religious Education, and Director of Religious Education at Girls and Boys Town in Omaha, Nebraska.

Author of more than forty articles and six books, Michael's work has appeared in a variety of publications. He regularly teaches graduate courses on adolescent spirituality and catechesis at Boston College, Loyola University of New Orleans, St. John's School of Theology in Minnesota, and Fordham University in New York.

WITH THANKS

We are grateful to the following seventh and eighth graders who all read the manuscript of this book, completed a written evaluation, and met with us to discuss it live. But most of all, we owe a debt of gratitude to their teacher, Stephanie Spiegel, M.Ed., who graciously and enthusiastically coordinated this effort.

7th and 8th Grade Religion Teacher, St. Vincent de Paul Elementary School

Stephanie Spiegel, M.Ed., B.A.

7th Grade Students

Maddy Amenta
Tiffany Anzalone
Maddy Becker
Michael Belford
Bryndan Broohm
Darren Chew
Madeline Clauff
Brittany DeWitt
Dylan Duren
Chad Elliott
Katy Feichtinger
TJ Feldhaus
Kaitlyn Fischer
Alex Frost
Becky Fuqua
Lauren Gentry
Kathleen Gerber
Carla Gibbs
Katherine Gould
Colin Hald
Steven Hanna
Tanner Hendricks
David Hollis
Abby Hughes
Lauren James
Anne Johnson
Mitchell Johnson
Alexis Kaiser
Kayla Kampschneider
Deirdre Kerins
Madeline LaHood
Casey Lavin
Katelin Lempka
Kyra Lindholm
Alexus Lodes
Zach Loeffelholz
Katie Luff
Paige Lynam
Quinn Maass
Philip Maschka
Caley Maszk
Claire McCarthy
Annie McClure
Matt McLeay
Scotty McLeay
Michael Meyers
Michael Mezzacappa
Rachel Mihulka

Hannah Miller
Christie Mitchell
Natalie Montanez
Allison Moran
Michael Morrison
Connor Mulhall
Emmett Nelson
Mikayla Neppl
Michaela O'Connor
Kevin Oldaker
Jozlyn Petsche
Abbey Podrazo
Erin Polito
Brad Prucha
Molly Rakoczy
Jake Rauterkus
Caitlyn Reilly
Lauren Ruden
Megan Rupiper
Sammy Salerno
Thomas Schleisman
Matthew Slump
Anna Smith
Michael Snow
Kelsie Stopak
Andrew Taylor
Dean Tiwald
Jackson Toner
Emily Vaiskunas
Michael Vankat
Nick Wentz
Jennifer Wiest
Emily Wilson
Chloe Wilwerding
William Wrich
Catherine Yost
Zach Zitek

8th Grade Students

Alex Augustyn
Andrea Alonso
Tristan Anzalone
Jillian Anderson
Max Barnes
Eric Binkley
Kath Borghoff
Jordan Bosilevac
Jen Bramhall
Tim Carlson
Alec Carstens
Dylan Carter
Danielle Christensen
Jack Clauff
Jack Colaric
Meghan Cronin
Jeff Crosson
Brian Delaney
Jake Denker
Alexander Duryea
Chelsey Eglseder
Sean Everson
Alexandra Fischer
Tyler Friend
Jenny Garvey
Thomas Gilgenast
Tim Gregg
Megan Hart
Eric Hofferber
Alicia Hoffmann
Corey Homan
Jared Homan
Travis Homan
Austin Jesz
Kathleen Kendall
Colton Kenney
Joe Kizer
Michaela Klesitz
Hailey Konnath
Raechel Kramer
Dana Kucirek
Cassidy Lemkau

John Linbo
Michael Maenner
Luke Maher
Scott Marsicek
Corinne McGill
Shannon McGill
Mike McKeone
Frank Mezzacappa
Alisa Muckey
Matt Nave
Caroline Nelsen
Emily Nelson
Brendan O'Byrne
Erin O'Loughlin
Michaela Onkka
Connor Orr
Adam Ossino
Teddy Pane
Sydney Pendergast
Ellie Pesavento
Will Pieper
Wade Pierce
Michael Pitner
Caitlyn Rathfon
Nick Revers
Gage Rohwer
Spencer Schofield
Nick Schwaller
Courtney Sehn
Molly Sova
Tom Spittler
Tyrel Spittler
Michael Stastny
Caleb Steffensmeier
Sam Sullivan
Will Suter
Daniel Tesarek
Eric Tesarek
Matthew Tesarek
Katelyn Thielen
Clare Tokheim
Lucas Vetter
Marie Wiggs
Alyssa Wilkie
Melody Yahnke

We also want to thank eighth graders Katherine Finn of Starlight, Indiana and Anthony Grasso of Elmwood Park, New Jersey for their written and verbal feedback early on.

LINCOLN PARK

Body and S.O.U.L.

Printed in the United States of America

ISBN 0-15-901905-2

1 2 3 4 5 6 076 12 11 10 09 08 07

THE TUNNEL

CHAPTER 1

MAYBE A LOT WEIRD

"The kids are on board."

"What kids?"

"The kids from Kennedy High, the Save Our Urban Life crowd."

"Carl, start over. I'm lost."

Carl Howard, the young administrative assistant to Chicago Councilwoman Martha Gray, stood in front of her desk. He was flipping pages in a spiral notebook, bringing her up to date.

"The Lincoln Park Tunnel Project."

He opened his eyes wider as if to say, "Remember?" But he didn't want to actually say that to his boss.

Councilwoman Martha Gray stopped signing papers and looked up, peering over her reading glasses.

"Go on," she said. Then she took off her glasses and gave him her total attention. Lincoln Park was a high priority.

The Lincoln Park Tunnel Project was part of the mayor's City Beautiful Campaign. There were six tunnels leading into the Lincoln Park Zoo. The tunnels were over sixty years-old, and corroding from the inside—filled with moss, mud, and mold. The caged lights along the tunnels' ceilings were either broken or burnt out; and people hurried through the tunnels as if they were trying to find their way out of a Halloween haunted forest. Each morning there were bags, cans, and broken bottles that needed to be cleaned up—traces of the previous night's visitors.

A million tourists a year walked through this mess to enter the last free zoo in the country, and an estimated 48 million dollars was spent at surrounding hotels, restaurants, and shops.

The mayor was blunt, "This is an embarrassment. Something has to be done."

The zoo was in Councilwoman Martha Gray's ward, and within a week of the mayor's remark, she had announced the Lincoln Park Tunnel Project. She had explained to everyone that fixing the tunnels of Lincoln Park was one way to make the zoo more attractive, and keep the money coming into the city. Business and hotel owners loved the idea. There had been a big press conference announcing the project. Every Chicago TV station had been there. The six tunnels would be kept clean and would be painted with murals, each with a different theme: *Great Americans*, *the World of Animals*, *Children Count*, *Workers of the World*, *Family Life*, and *Spiritual Heritage*.

The word went out. Six artists were hired, and all agreed to finish the tunnels by the end of August. It was now early September.

"You said you wanted community organizations to rally around the project," Carl went on. "Yesterday, I talked to a young teacher at Kennedy High School. Her name is Jamie Allister. She sponsors an after-school service club called Save Our Urban Life, SOUL for short. She says that she can get her students to clean up the park and the tunnels almost every month. She says that it fits in with their mission statement."

"What is their mission statement?" Councilwoman Gray inquired.

"I made the same mistake of asking. When she told me, I had her say it a second time, very slowly, so I could write it down."

Carl flipped to the back of his spiral notebook. He wanted to make sure he got it right.

"We seek to serve urban life, not only the human, but plants, animals, the earth, and anything else living in or beyond the mysterious universe."

A light bulb went on in Councilwoman Gray's political brain. She was on her feet. "This is good! Youthful idealism! This gives us the angle we need. Let's portray it as 'the future investing in the future.' That kind of thing. It'll make the mayor happy. And it will keep those tunnels from becoming an embarrassment."

Martha Gray was satisfied. She turned back toward the desk and offhandedly asked, "Are all the tunnels finished?"

"Well, er . . . yes," Carl replied.

She stopped and turned back toward Carl. She was a veteran politician and could catch a problem in the tone of voice or the slightest of stammers.

"Out with it," she demanded.

Carl swallowed hard, "Well, I was in the park over the weekend and checked out the tunnels. All of them are done, but one of them is a little weird."

"A little weird?"

Carl swallowed hard a second time, "Maybe a lot weird?"

"Which one?"

"The Spiritual Heritage Tunnel."

"What do you mean by 'a lot weird'?"

"You'd better see it."

CHAPTER 2

A PUZZLE OF A TUNNEL

"Oh, my heavens! Oh, my heavens! What is all this?" Councilwoman Gray gasped.

She was turning around and around, looking at the different images painted all over the tunnel. Her mouth was wide open, and her hands were up in the air.

"Maybe that's it. Maybe it's heaven!" Carl said, trying to agree with his boss.

She dropped her hands to her side and exhaled slowly, trying to calm down.

Every inch of the inside of the Spiritual Heritage Tunnel was painted. The walkway itself, including the metal drain cover, was painted—as a strip of brown earth splitting a reddish sea with a huge wall of waves on each side. The ceiling of the tunnel was a brilliant blue, covered with everything that flies—an eagle, a hawk, a raven, a parrot, a swarm of bees, an owl, a pair of vultures, a giant monarch butterfly, and a dove that gave the definite impression that it was descending.

"Where am I?" she said, half in confusion and half in desperation.

"You might be standing in the Red Sea," Carl replied, pointing down to her feet. One foot appeared to be on dry ground and the other in the splashing waves.

"But I can't tell for sure. No Moses," he added.

On the walls were too many images to take in at once: a pyramid with an open eye in the middle; a burning bush; a lotus floating on the water; a she-wolf nursing two pups; a cross with jewels on it; a great white bear laying on its side and playfully twirling a crown; a shepherd's staff with flowers blooming on its handle; a chalice floating in midair and radiating light; a dancing woman with three sets of arms; a couple of peacocks; a pearl surrounded by more water; a crescent moon; a five-pointed star; a cave with a wide, dark opening; a child juggling stars; a pregnant woman dressed in blue and wearing a black arm band; and a giraffe in full gallop.

"What's that?!" Councilwoman Gray yelled, pointing at the far end of the tunnel.

She and Carl walked over, leaned down, and looked closely.

"A snake," Carl answered.

"What's it doing?"

"Shedding its skin, I think," he replied.

"Lovely."

Martha Gray took another look around the tunnel, this time more slowly.

"Where are the churches? The synagogues? The mosques?

Where are the priests, ministers, and rabbis? Where are the *people*? Where are people praying over gravesites, chaplains at battlefields, or men and women at the bedside of elderly loved ones in hospitals? How about a banner with 'One Nation Under God'?"

Then she paused and, in her best councilwoman voice, asked, "There's nothing dirty in here, is there?"

She and Carl scanned the walls one more time. They didn't see any unmentionable body parts.

"Who's the artist?" she asked.

Carl had the file in his hands, "OrSo."

"Call him . . . her."

"Well, I thought you might want to meet this artist, so I tried. But we can't get a hold of him . . . her," Carl said.

"Is it a man or a woman?"

"Don't know," said Carl.

"Who hired the artist?"

Carl spoke in a low voice, knowing he was delivering more bad news. "Not sure exactly. Anyway, the address he . . . she gave us turns out to be a playground near a high school."

He paused.

"And the telephone turns out to be a pay phone."

Martha Gray leaned against the tunnel wall for support.

"Let me get it straight. We hired an artist who may be a man or may be a woman, but who nevertheless painted this insane collection of animals and symbols that somehow is supposed to represent our spiritual heritage. And we have no way of contacting him or her?"

"Correct," Carl replied, looking down at his shoes.

"Has anyone complained?" Martha inquired.

Carl shook his head. "Negative."

"Okay. Here's how we'll handle it. Issue a statement thanking all the artists. Find some phrasing that says the talented artists went well beyond the committee's expectations, and proved the old saying about artistic creativity having no limits. This way we cover ourselves if someone complains. We can chalk it up to an overenthusiastic artist."

Carl was silent for a moment. "You know, Martha, I think it's kinda cool."

"Carl, you brought me out here because you told me, and I quote, 'It's weird.'"

"Weird but meaningful. Betcha all these figures stand for something," he said.

"Yeah, right," said Ms. Gray. "Maybe there's too much meaning."

Carl just looked at her. He knew the wheels were turning.

Both were silent. Finally, she laughed and said, "As long as we're in the Spiritual Heritage Tunnel, I think we should pray."

"Pray for what?" he asked.

"Pray that this weird tunnel is not part of a larger puzzle."

KATE

CHAPTER 3

BOUNCING

"You gotta do what?"

"I gotta join a club!"

"You gotta whaaat???"

Mrs. DiGiacomo could hardly hear her daughter's voice over the rumble of the clothes dryer. It was the Sunday night ritual—wash and dry last week's laundry, so that everyone would have fresh, clean clothes for the upcoming week of school. Each Sunday Mrs. D turned into a laundry maniac, grumbling to herself in disbelief, as she attacked the clothes piles like a madwoman.

Towards the end of the summer, the piles had started growing, and the majority of the clothes belonged to 14-year-old Kate DiGiacomo. Kate had begun freshman year with quite the back-to-school wardrobe, but that hadn't stopped her weekend splurges at the mall. She'd been spending her allowance and babysitting earnings on nothing but more clothes, more shoes, and more jewelry.

Kate walked into the laundry room with still more clothes and dropped them in front of the washer. Mrs. D was bent over a pile of darks, mostly green and denim.

"I just don't see why you need ten pairs of jeans and eight green shirts, Kate! They all look the same," Mrs. D sighed, scooping the load up and into the washing machine.

"No they don't, Mom. Besides, green's my favorite color."

Mrs. D poured the soap into the wash and turned on the machine, glancing to see Kate's most recent heap of clothes on the floor. "I'm not washing those. I told you to make sure all of the laundry was here this morning," she said, annoyed.

"I know. *I'll* wash them, ok? I forgot about them. They were in my overnight bag from when I spent the night at Brianna's," Kate replied.

Mrs. D took a deep breath and remembered that Kate had been trying to ask her a question.

"Now what were you saying you *gotta* do?"

"I have to join an extracurricular club at school. It's a freshman rule. And I don't know which one I should join," Kate said, a hint of a question.

Mrs. D was surprised that her daughter was actually talking to her about school stuff. It was rare, like a solar eclipse. Nevertheless, Mrs. D couldn't resist a little laundry room sarcasm, "Join one where you can wear sweats, instead of expensive jeans."

Kate rolled her eyes and quickly turned to head for the stairs.

"Hold on, just kidding," Mrs. D said, as she put her arm around Kate's shoulders.

Together they went into the kitchen and sat down at the table.

"So what are your choices?"

"Students Against Drunk Driving, Yearbook, Hospital Helpers, Save Our Urban Life, and School Dances . . . Oh, and I can join Key Club, as long as my grades stay good."

"And your grades *will* stay good!"

"This is why I never ask for advice."

"Fair enough. So what seems interesting to you? Or fun?"

"I dunno."

"What's everyone else doing?"

"Everybody's doing something different."

Just then, 12-year-old Eric DiGiacomo made one of his grand entrances, coming into the kitchen with his fly unzipped.

"Supper?" he asked innocently.

"Ten minutes," replied Mrs. D, holding all ten fingers outstretched in front of her face.

"Good. Smells GREAT!" Eric sniffed the air.

"Eric?"

"Yah?"

Mrs. D pointed down at his pants. He laughed and zipped them up.

"Go wash your hands and then you can set the table for us, ok?"

"Ok!" Eric extended his arms out like an airplane and zoomed out of the kitchen.

Mrs. D smiled at her son's joy. Kate rolled her eyes.

"He's never going to grow up!" Kate complained in frustration.

Her little brother's Down's Syndrome got on her nerves more and more lately. It wasn't such a big deal when he was a little kid, because he did normal kid stuff. Now that he was in the seventh grade, it wasn't so cute anymore.

"Is it *always* going to bother you?" asked Mrs. D.

"I dunno," Kate said as she headed to her room.

She plunked down on her bed and began to fold a pile of clothes. Kate couldn't deny it any longer—Eric was really bothering her. Disrupting her life. Embarrassing her on a constant basis.

He looked like he was from another planet. His clothes were totally out of style, wrinkled, and too small. Half the time they didn't even match. He always forgot to button his shirt. His hair was messy and not in a cool, bed head sort of way. At school, he looked out of place. Kate was glad that she had finally graduated junior high. Now that she was at Kennedy High, she didn't have to be humiliated all day, every day. She loved him, but she hated being seen with him. He looked like a misfit. He looked like a dork. He looked *retarded*.

"Supper!" announced Eric as he stuck his head inside Kate's room.

A sense of guilt flooded her at the sight of his sweet, smiling face.

"Great!" said Kate, as she bounded off her bed and playfully slapped her brother's chest. She ruffled his hair as they headed down the stairs toward the kitchen.

For a second, Kate saw deep inside herself, and realized she was always bouncing between self-conscious embarrassment and outright love for her little brother. She wondered if it would ever stop.

CHAPTER 4

GLAMOUR GIRL

"I say you join Yearbook," Mrs. D said to Kate after praying the blessing before supper.

"I dunno," Kate replied as she helped Eric load his plate with a heap of Greek salad. He immediately began picking the cucumbers and black olives out, making separate piles designated for each food.

"You'd learn a lot."

"I don't want to learn anything more. I've got too much to learn already."

"But you'd learn how to edit . . . how to do page layout . . . maybe some graphic design stuff . . . things you'll never study in class."

"Salad's great, Mom!" said Eric with another one of his big smiles. He reached across the table to grab a hunk of bread, just missing his glass of milk. Kate sighed as Eric looked up at her, grinned, and took a big bite.

"Yeah, but if you're on Yearbook you have to do a lot of work," Kate said, turning her attention back to her mom. "There's like deadlines and stuff. You can't be late with your assignments at all. I already have a ton of homework!"

"I just think it would be a valuable experience," Mrs. D concluded.

"I dunno," Kate said.

Everyone was quiet as they finished their salads.

"Let me ask you a question, Kate," asked Mrs. D as she began serving each of them a generous portion of her famous enchilada casserole.

"What?" asked Kate, not noticing the mischievous twinkle in her mother's eyes until it was too late.

"Why don't you start the Glamour Girl Shopaholics' Club? No homework, no learning, just clothes and jewelry!" Mrs. D kidded her daughter.

"Ha! Shopaholics. Ha! Ha!" laughed Eric as he nodded in agreement.

"Very funny," Kate conceded.

After supper, it was Eric's turn to clear the table, and Kate's turn to watch him. He didn't need any help that evening. He walked around and around the table picking up each item one at a time. Forks first and over to the sink. Knives. Spoons. Plates. Glasses. The salad bowl and casserole dish came last. Kate didn't mind so much this evening that it took him forever. He finished by opening the dishwasher so that Mrs. D could load it up later, after she had tucked them in.

"Good job!" Kate was always proud of him when he remembered that last step.

Eric turned and gave Kate two thumbs up.

"So I'm a shopaholic, huh?" Kate teased.

"And a Jewelry Queen," he added with a nod and a smile.

"And a what?!" she asked, shocked by the title he had invented for her.

"Jewelry Queen," he repeated without a second of hesitation. Then he placed his hand on his ears and got specific. "Earrings" . . . moved his hands to his throat and added, "Necklaces" . . . placed his hands on his waist, "Belts". . . grabbed one wrist with his other hand, "Bracelets". . . bent over and touched his toes, "Toe rings". . . touched his ankles, "Ankle bracelets". . . then held out his fingers, wiggled them in his sister's face and finished with "Finger rings."

"What, you don't like my stuff?" Kate asked.

Eric just shrugged his shoulders as if to say, "I don't know." Maybe even "I don't care." He had explained what he had meant by Jewelry Queen. He was done now and headed for the TV.

Kate went into the laundry room. Taking the clothes out of the dryer and placing them in an empty basket, she noticed that most of the clothes *were* hers. Not to mention the clothes she'd already folded. She shoved the load of almost all jeans and green shirts into the dryer. She *did* have enough clothes for three well-dressed girls, but she had just started life in high school and had to make a good impression. A first impression was a lasting impression, and the first thing her friends noticed was how much you styled. Or didn't.

Kate poured the detergent into the washing machine and started the small load from her overnight bag. The sleepover had been great. Kate, Brianna, Jen, and Caitlyn had indulged in one too many scoops of cookie dough ice cream; they spent the night listening to CDs, flipping through celebrity and fashion magazines, playing with new hairstyles, and trying on new make-up.

Thinking of her friends reminded her that she needed to decide on a club by homeroom tomorrow. She finished her Algebra homework and then slipped in a few calls before bed. She called Caitlyn, then Jen, and then Brianna. Three phone calls and thirty minutes later, she had her decision.

"Cool," she said to herself, hanging up the phone and switching off the bedside lamp.

On the way to school the next morning, Eric was riding shotgun, chatting away.

Kate was in the backseat, snoring.

"First stop," Mrs. D announced as she pulled up to the curb at Kennedy High and woke up Kate.

"Have a good one, Kate," she said.

"You, too," said Kate as she shook off her stupor and fumbled for her backpack.

"Have a nice day," echoed Eric.

"You, too," smiled Kate.

"HEY!" yelled Mrs. D as Kate stepped onto the sidewalk. "Which club?"

"SOUL," Kate turned around to answer.

"SOUL?"

"Save Our Urban Life," said Kate.

"Why?" asked Mrs. D, not noticing the mischievous look on her daughter's face until it was too late.

Kate stuck her head back into the car, smiled big, and, as she squeezed Eric's cheek, chuckled, "Cute guys!"

ROBBIE

CHAPTER 5

LIFTING...AND THE OTHER THING

"Robbie ? . . ."

"Roooooobbie?"

"Hello, Robbie?"

"Anybody home?"

Upstairs in his bedroom, freshman Robbie Matthews was sitting in front of his computer and talking on his cell. The music was vibrating so loud that the speakers were wiggling on the bookshelf above his desk. He never heard his uncle come inside the house, or up the stairs to his bedroom. If he had heard Uncle Shaun calling, he would have minimized the window on his computer screen.

"Yeah, I got the link," Robbie said to his buddy, Carlos.

"WHAT THE . . . !" yelled Uncle Shaun, as he stepped into the room and saw what was on the computer screen.

"Carlos, I'll call you later. Gotta go."

Robbie clicked off his cell with one hand, and lowered the volume of his computer with the other hand. He had been caught. Red-handed. Busted for looking at porn.

Uncle Shaun glared at the computer. He rubbed at his forehead with his fingers as if he was trying hard to think about the right way to approach the issue.

"This is wrong, Robbie! Way wrong!"

Robbie was too embarrassed to speak. His voice was locked inside his throat. He could feel his face turning red, hot and flushed.

"Man, Robbie! First, there was that magazine and now this. I mean girls can look hot and whatever, but man, you have got to learn to draw the line. What's going on here?"

Robbie remembered the magazine. The last time Uncle Shaun showed up, he had spotted a bodybuilding magazine falling from Robbie's backpack. On the cover there were two women in skimpy bikinis. But it was nothing like the magazine that was now stashed under his mattress, the magazine Carlos had given him.

"Robbie, talk to me. Say something. Say *anything*!" Shaun wanted an explanation.

He used that phrase, "Say *anything*" on purpose and Robbie knew it. He knew exactly what it meant.

Robbie's mother, Uncle Shaun's big sister, had died of cancer two years ago. Toward the end, when she knew she wasn't going to make it, she would always ask Robbie and Shaun to make her a promise: "Never stop talking to each other. Okay? And promise me, you'll *say anything.*" She must have asked Robbie and Shaun to make this promise about ten different times before she died. But Robbie never guessed "*anything*" would be so hard.

"I was over at Carlos' house awhile back," Robbie started slowly. "It was around lunch so we pigged out on leftover pizza, watched a movie on TV, shot some hoops in the driveway. By two we were bored. Carlos asked me if I wanted to see something. We went up to his room. He locked the door, reached under the mattress of his bed, and pulled out a magazine that we looked at. Then he said, 'That's nothing,' and turned on his computer. I know a lot about computer stuff, but I had never gone there until Carlos showed me."

Robbie stopped talking.

"Are you blaming Carlos?" Shaun was not going to let him off the hook.

"No."

Robbie had no more words.

"How long have you been looking at this stuff?" Shaun wanted more.

"Just for like the last five minutes."

"You know what I mean," said Shaun, shaking his head.

"Most of the summer," Robbie admitted.

"So, you've been scoping out porn for over a month?"

"Yes," Robbie said quietly.

Shaun got quiet for a couple of seconds, which seemed longer to Robbie.

"That stuff is dehumanizing, Robbie. Women aren't sex objects. What if one of those ladies was your mom? I mean, your sister?" Shaun swallowed hard.

It wasn't the smartest thing to come out of his mouth.

"The more you mess with that kind of stuff, the more it gets inside your head. And it's not good for your mind. It's not good for your soul. Man Robbie, people get addicted to that stuff. It can be like drugs."

Then, in a quiet and exasperated voice, he said, "You've got to stop."

Robbie, who had been looking at the floor, nodded.

Shaun wanted to change the topic and get things back to normal. He noticed a big plastic container of powdered whey protein on Robbie's dresser.

"You still lifting?" asked Shaun as he gestured with his chin towards the container of powder that weightlifters used to bulk up.

"Nonstop."

Robbie had started on the weights, as soon as he had finished eighth grade.

"How many times a week are you in the gym?" asked Uncle Shaun.

"Three, sometimes more," Robbie answered.

"All weights? Or cardio, too?"

"No cardio. Just serious lifting."

"Lifting is good for you so long as you do it right. You aren't overdoing it, are you? Not lifting *too* much?"

"Nah."

"Seriously Robbie, you're only fourteen. Your body's gonna change no matter what you do, so don't overdo it. You're tall and skinny, but that's going to change."

Shaun started heading for the door. They had talked enough. They had said *something* and *anything*. But Shaun couldn't resist one last lesson. He stopped abruptly and looked Robbie square in the eyes.

"Question of the day. You know what porn and weightlifting have in common?"

"No."

"The BODY, man, the BODY! Maybe you got this body thing going on. Seems like you're awfully focused on it these days—your muscles, and naked ladies."

Just then, Robbie's cell phone rang. Out of habit, Robbie glanced at the Caller ID.

"It's dad. Should I get it?"

"You understand what I'm telling you about this body thing?" asked Shaun.

"I think so."

"Go on then. Tell your dad to give me a call, too."

Robbie worried about what Uncle Shaun wanted to say to his father.

CHAPTER 6

STOCKS, DINNER, AND DAD

"What's the market doing?" Mr. Matthews asked.

"Started with a dip—a big dip, actually—but it recovered by the end of day," said Robbie.

"How did your stocks do?"

"Pretty good."

"Any advice for me?"

"You'll be fine. The blue chips are slow, but they're steady. Be patient," Robbie explained.

"Thanks. Gotta go. See you in an hour."

"Okay, Dad. Tonight it's pasta," Robbie replied.

Two years ago Robbie's dad had bought him a laptop, and had given him two thousand dollars to invest. About the same time Robbie's mom died of cancer. Robbie's two thousand was now five thousand. Robbie went online and checked the market every day after school. His dad liked to check in with him for some free advice now and then.

Robbie started the water boiling for the pasta. He poured a jar of spaghetti sauce into a pan and put the heat on low.

"Gotta fix this," he said to himself, referring to the spaghetti sauce in a jar. He turned up the music, and then he started adding stuff to the sauce: garlic powder, basil (which he rubbed in his hands first to help it come alive), a pinch of oregano, some olive oil, and a bit of grated cheese. He stirred it all into the sauce and kept the heat on low. Then he took out half a stick of butter and put it on the counter.

"Need to add some of this at the end," he told himself.

He had learned to cook by watching his mother. Getting supper ready for his dad and him always made Robbie feel close to her. He set the table as the pasta water heated up.

After she died, Robbie and his dad ate dinner together as often as they could.

It took about twenty minutes more to cook the pasta. Mr. Matthews showed up a few minutes after that.

"Sauce is good!" said Mr. Matthews after washing up and sitting down at the kitchen table.

Robbie nodded in agreement as he tried to get the spaghetti dangling from his mouth into his stomach.

"You had a good day at the stock market. How about school?"

"Good," gulped Robbie. "We had to sign up for after-school stuff today."

"What do you mean?"

"Like extracurricular activities and stuff."

"Trying out for basketball, right?"

"Nope," Robbie said, with more pasta in his mouth.

"Why not? You've got the height!"

"Not a ballplayer."

"You're only a freshman. You got two years to develop yourself!"

"You sound just like the coaches."

"Think ahead, Robbie. Your body will take you there."

These were the moments when Robbie hated his body the most. His body seemed to rule his life: *Since you're six feet four inches, you have to hoop it up; since you're so skinny, you have to lift.* He wasn't the one that decided to be so tall, but he was stuck with it, and all the stuff that came with it. That's why he liked the stock market and cooking. His body didn't matter.

"Dad, I think ahead all the time with the stock market, don't I? Besides, I'm not a ballplayer," Robbie repeated.

Then, with a mouth full of pasta, he added, "Maybe I'm a chef."

As his father laughed, Robbie got up his courage. "Uncle Shaun was looking for you about an hour ago. He said to call him."

"Oh that's right!" said Mr. Matthews.

"I was supposed to get home a little early today. He and I were going to start looking for his tux."

"I need one too, right?"

"Yup. You're both in the wedding party, so that means tuxes," nodded Mr. Matthews. "This sauce is really good Robbie." He added. "What did Uncle Shaun have to say? Anything?"

"Not much. He was reminding me about how to lift and

stuff," Robbie didn't dare mention the other stuff.

It got really quiet as Robbie and his dad finished dinner.

"Back to school . . . if you aren't trying out for basketball, what *did* you sign up for?" Mr. M finally asked.

"Some group, Save Our Planet or something. They call it SOUL. All I know is that it only meets once a month. And they do stuff outside."

THE STORY OF SOUL

CHAPTER 7

LEGENDS

"Tell me about the Great One."

"You want to know about who?" 50-year-old Katherine Allister stopped putting away the groceries, and looked at her 24-year-old daughter sitting at the kitchen table.

"Alexander the Great."

"You mean Lucan?"

"Yeah, the Great One."

Jamie Allister was in her second year of teaching social studies at Kennedy High School. She was also the moderator for Save Our Urban Life, the very same club her mother had belonged to "back in the day"—as her students called it. Jamie's mom could not tell old high school stories without mentioning the club and its chief founder, Alexander Lucan. He, along with two other students, Elise Waters and Tony "Stick" Happold, had started the club in 1971.

Besides the fact that they had founded SOUL, there was very little known about them. Elise had joined the Peace Corps after graduating from Kennedy and was said to still be teaching children to read in Somalia. After high school, Stick got drafted and went to Vietnam where he was reported missing in action a year later. Alexander Lucan's family had left Chicago and moved to California right after graduation. None of them had ever attended any of the school reunions.

"We start again on Wednesday, and I want to tell the new kids about how the club got started. I'd also like to give the older kids some inside stories from someone who was actually there," Jamie told her mom.

Katherine Allister stopped shelving the groceries and sat down. Her daughter needed some of *the juice*, as Stick used to say. She had told her daughter some of the founding stories, but now Jamie wanted more. Always a good sign. But she didn't need to know everything. Stories, but not the whole story. Katherine would only give her a few tidbits from the legendary past. More would come later, in due course, when Jamie was ready.

"Alexander Lucan was normal. Not brilliant. Not funny. Just normal. But on the other hand, he was different. He was a puzzle nerd, dabbled in painting, messed around with poetry . . ."

"Mom, how about the important thing. What did he look like?"

"Want to see pictures?"

"Absolutely!"

Katherine went to the basement and came back minutes later with the 1971 Kennedy High yearbook. It was royal blue with "The K" written in huge white letters across the cover.

"Here's Tony Happold, Alexander Lucan, and Elise Waters . . . in alphabetical order," Katherine said as she slowly cracked open the three different pages.

"Oh my," Jamie said softly, as the legends appeared, one by one, at her mother's kitchen table.

She had imagined them to be bigger than life, mythic characters, like out of some book you studied in English Lit class.

"They were just kids," Jaime said quietly.

"We all were," Katherine said. "Nothing wrong with being a kid."

"Can I bring this to school with me?"

"Anything to help. Now back to what really matters."

Katherine smiled at her daughter, who smiled back. Point taken.

"SOUL was started by the kids who were always asking questions no one ever thought of," Katherine said.

"Questions?" Jamie asked.

"Yeah. I still remember the questions they asked about the way the news portrayed social activists or how the media *didn't* give coverage to activists . . . like Cesar Chavez, who worked to help migrant farmers get fair pay. In fact, the SOUL kids were the only ones in school who wondered about media bias. Nowadays, it's something everyone talks about," Katherine explained.

"So they were thinkers."

Katherine nodded and kept talking. "We were still in the Vietnam War, so everyone was paying attention to that, making noise about it, actually."

"Were you into the Vietnam War protest?" Jamie asked.

"Not really. See, here's another example," Katherine pointed at the caption saying "No meat for me until the rainforests are free!" beneath a photo of Alexander Lucan.

"Lucan and the others were raising questions about how the fast-food hamburger chains were destroying the rainforest in order to raise cows."

"So you guys were into things that no one else was paying attention to?"

"Paying attention is the key to SOUL. That's how they came up with Save Our Urban Life. American society was focused on two or three big issues—the War on Poverty, civil rights, Vietnam—which were really important. But there were little local issues that were also important."

"And these were issues that high school kids could get involved in. Make a difference," Jamie concluded.

"Exactly," Katherine smiled.

"So the founders of the club were thinkers," Jamie repeated.

"And doers!" Katherine exclaimed.

"Like what? What did you *do*?" Jamie asked.

"We visited people in hospitals who didn't have anyone to visit them, and played cards and checkers with them. We taught reading to kids and to some adults who were having trouble getting it. We started clean-up projects in our neighborhoods, and volunteered for clean-ups in other neighborhoods." Katherine paused, "And we held babies."

"What was *that* about?" Jamie said with a hint of surprise in her voice.

"In those days there were orphanages that had nurseries with babies who had been abandoned or given away at birth. These nurseries needed people to come in and just hold the babies, nothing else. The nurses supervised us. We just sat in chairs and held babies. Skin contact. No words. Just thoughts. We knew it was good for the babies and good for us. We were always concerned about the soul. Babies help bring it out."

"Speaking of souls," Jamie said, "no one got a coin last year."

CHAPTER 8

THE COIN

"It's not easy to get a coin. Besides, you don't get one—you receive one."

Katherine Allister got up from the table and began to pace.

Jamie knew the beginning of a lecture when she saw one, and she had heard this lecture before.

"Mom, I know this already. I was in SOUL, remember?"

Katherine Allister was like an entirely different woman whenever she talked about SOUL. She was no longer a tired mother putting away boxes and cans. She was a spiritual teacher handing on a tradition. She ignored her daughter's attempt to put on the brakes.

"The coin symbolizes the secret center of Save Our Urban Life. It's part of what you see and what you don't see. What you see—what everybody on the outside sees—is kids taking on issues that deal with urban life. What you don't see is what is happening to the kids who begin to *pay attention*. The kids open up in ways they never dreamed of. They discover their souls! The coin is also the symbol of what you don't see, the spiritual awakening, what we used to call 'the stuff that really matters.' To receive a coin means you're on the path. We took the *coin* out of *coin*cidence, because we didn't think there were any coincidences. Everything is secretly tied together. You still with me?"

Jamie hadn't seen a coin in five years. Some of her classmates had received coins during their senior year at Kennedy, when they were all in SOUL together. But she remembered clearly what the coin looked like.

The bronze-looking coin was the size of a quarter but thin like a dime. On one side, there was a figure like an angel, and around the figure the words *Truth, Beauty, Love*. On the other side, the letters *S, O, U, and L* were stamped in the middle, and the words *See, Judge, Act* were inscribed around them.

"You receive a coin if you recognize and follow Truth, Beauty, or Love into a deeper level of spirit," her mother continued. "Or if you have seen, judged, and acted in a way that enriches the Spirit of another person. Both these things—taking responsibility for your spiritual awakening and helping enrich the Spirit of others—are how you attend to the soul. Two sides of the same coin. Get it?"

"And if you receive a coin, you have to give it away," Jamie finished, mimicking the slow cadence of her mother's speech.

"That's right," her mother said, ignoring Jamie's imitation. "What you receive, you give. You find someone else who is on the path of the soul, not just on the outside, but on the inside."

"Mom, I've heard all this. I need to know more."

"Even if you knew more, there would still be more to know."

Jamie gave her mother a look. When her mother got like this, everything seemed to go around in circles. But Jamie wanted more information for her students, so she kept pushing.

"Why isn't any of this soul and coin stuff written down?" she asked.

"It's an oral tradition."

"What if it's forgotten?" Jamie pressed on.

"Writing stuff down doesn't mean it will automatically be remembered. It only makes sure it's recorded," Katherine explained.

"Can you tell other people about the coin?" Jamie asked.

"When you know what to say," replied Katherine.

"When do you know what to say?"

"When you know what you have received."

Jamie was chasing her mother in circles. "Mom, how can I tell my students about SOUL when I don't know as much as you?"

"Tell them all you know. Then tell them there is a lot more you don't know."

"I'll lose credibility." The secret fear of all young teachers was exposed.

"What will you gain?" asked her mother.

The question took Jaime by surprise. But she had the answer instantly. She didn't have to think about it. It was in her mouth before she knew it.

"Honesty," Jamie said, and laughed out loud at how obvious it was.

Her mother laughed back.

"As long as I'm being honest, there's more I want to tell you, Mom."

CHAPTER 9

GETTING TOUGHER

"Last year was my first year, and I had no idea what I was doing. This year I'm cracking down. I made meeting rules, and I didn't invite last year's ninth graders back. I'm getting tougher." It was Jamie's turn to pace while her mother sat at the table.

Katherine Allister not only heard words. She heard beneath them.

"Are you getting tough because no coins appeared?" she asked.

"What else?"

"Are you blaming the kids or yourself?"

"A little of both," Jamie admitted.

"Suppose you blamed less and learned more?"

"Meaning what?"

"Instead of trying to figure out who to blame right away, stay with the mistakes longer, until you can learn from them," Katherine explained.

As long as Jamie could remember, this had been her mother's message. Whenever anything went wrong, mom would find the lesson in it. If the lesson wasn't obvious, mom would wait until it appeared. She believed people acted too quickly. She thought they should wait for the whole situation to present itself.

"That may be fine for little things. But when you're in charge, you have a responsibility to root out the ones that are goofing off," said Jamie, a year's teaching experience under her belt.

"Give it a try, Jamie. Kids aren't the only ones who have to learn."

Enough mother and daughter fencing. They had debated with each other long enough. After the occasional match, they were always quiet. Words had done what they could. Now there was silence.

Finally Katherine said, "Sit down. I have some news."

Jamie sat down and gave her mother a curious look.

"Remember how I made an appointment with Dr. Lyndhurst? When I was having female problems—all that pain and cramping?"

"Yes," Jamie said hesitantly, fearing what was coming.

"Well, looks like I need an operation."

"Oh my gosh. What kind of operation?"

"A hysterectomy. Standard procedure. So don't worry!" Katherine locked eyes with Jamie, smiled reassuringly, and continued, "No more having babies for me. Time for me to find different ways to give birth. Maybe it's time . . ."

"WHEN?!!"

"A week from this Saturday, first thing in the morning."

"How serious is it? Is it. . .?" Jamie couldn't bring herself to say the word.

"Cancer? Thankfully, no. The doctor says that my uterus has got to come out. Benign tumors, not cancerous ones. It's a routine surgery, and I promise I will be back to my old healthy self soon. No biggie!"

"But Mom, it is a big deal!"

"Jamie, relax. It's common for women my age. No big thing. Trust me," Katherine said.

"I'll go with you, mom. I'll stay over that Friday night and drive you to the hospital in the morning," offered Jamie.

"Isn't that Saturday, the day of your first SOUL event?"

"Well, yeah. But that won't be a problem. I'll cancel it, or get another teacher to take them."

"So what's the project?" asked Katherine.

"We're scheduled to go to Lincoln Park. Kind of a fall cleaning thing connected to the park's new tunnel program. The city has made a big investment into restoring the park and the zoo and stuff."

"I heard about that," said Katherine. "I heard that they had repainted all the tunnels with murals. Some of them are supposed to be really amazing."

"Mom, stop changing the subject!"

"Well, sounds like SOUL needs you! Dad is in town that weekend. He'll be with me. You can visit me after the operation, in the afternoon, when you're done."

"No, I'm going to get someone else to supervise the kids

that day."

"If you don't work with them, Jamie, souls will sleep."

Jamie was still upset. Her stomach was in knots. But her mother was right.

"Sometimes when we have these talks, I wonder where my practical, no-nonsense mother goes to, and what wild mystic has replaced her," Jamie said.

Katherine Allister was finding a new way to give birth to her daughter. She smiled, leaned over, and kissed Jamie in the middle of her forehead, between her two green-gray eyes. Right where the potential of the soul sleeps.

CHAPTER 10

TELLING IT LIKE IT IS

"All right, settle down," Jamie Allister announced in her typical teacher voice. She waited for everyone to get quiet.

The first meeting of SOUL was only two minutes old, and Alvin Kline, an overeager ninth grader, had his hand up for the third time.

Ms. Allister nodded in his direction.

"Do we get a grade for this?" Alvin was prepared to rattle off his usual questions, his specialty ever since he was in grade school. His pen was poised.

The whole group groaned.

"No grades, Alvin. This isn't a class . . . But there might be tests," said Ms. A.

Alvin looked puzzled. No grade. Not a class. But tests?

Then, before Alvin could raise his hand again, Ms. A looked at senior officers Ben Alvarez and Dana Calli, nodding her head slightly.

"We have two goals this year," Ben announced.

Dana chimed in, "The zoo at Lincoln Park and . . ."

Before she could finish, the room erupted.

"The zoo??!!!" someone said loudly.

"Sounds like we're the new poop scoop squad," laughed a junior.

"NO way are we going to the zoo! My little brother goes to the zoo!" exclaimed a senior.

"Do we have to bathe the boa constrictors?" joked the junior.

"How 'bout washing down elephants?" laughed someone at the back of the room.

Ms. Allister knew this would be the way the returning members of SOUL would react. She had learned a lot last year. This year she was ready. She had made a poster during her free period before lunch. Now she stood up and taped it to the board, without saying a word. It got everyone's attention.

Four Meeting Rules

Say Anything (appropriately)
One Person at a Time
No Put-Downs
Participate, Participate, Participate!

"My bad," someone admitted.

"Sorry," said another.

Dana continued, "We've been asked to help out with the new City Beautiful Campaign this year."

"Actually, we've been assigned to help maintain Lincoln Park, which mostly involves keeping the zoo straight. In particular, we have to take care of the tunnels," Ben explained.

"This is more serious than you think. The Lincoln Park Zoo is one of the country's only free zoos. People who come to Chicago make a point of checking it out," Dana added.

"Plus, it fits our mission," said Ben.

Ms. Allister nodded again, this time to seniors Derrick Lamay and Ellen Linh, who started distributing handouts, as if the whole presentation had been rehearsed.

"It's probably a good idea if we take a few minutes to remind ourselves of the purpose of Save Our Urban Life, and to welcome the new freshmen who have joined us," said Ms. A. "They need to become familiar with this as well. So, let's all take a minute to read it."

Kennedy High's Save Our Urban Life

Save Our Urban Life (SOUL) was started in 1971 here at Kennedy High by three seniors—Tony Happold, Alexander Lucan, and Elise Waters. It was a time of huge national unrest: the Vietnam War, the Hippie Movement, Woodstock Generation, civil rights, the War on Poverty, and so forth.

The founders wrote a simple mission statement: *We seek to serve urban life, not only the human, but plants, animals, the earth, and anything else living in or beyond the mysterious universe.*

Several underclassmen joined them that first year. Some say that the last phrase, *living in or beyond*

> *the mysterious universe*, made this group different. It gave the group a certain edge, and it attracted a lot of different kinds of students.
>
> For some unknown reason, Kennedy's Save Our Urban Life group caught on at other high schools across the country. Today, there are 1,285 SOULs throughout the United States. It's much like Students Against Drunk Driving (SADD), except that most Save Our Urban Life groups are found in big-city high schools where students come face to face with the issues, concerns, and treasures of urban environments.

Ms. A waited until the last head had looked up from the page. Then she began by saying, "There's more. Even more than I know. What I know I will tell you."

She looked around. Far from losing credibility, like she had feared, the students seemed interested. Everyone sat frozen in their seats, ready to hear what she had to say.

She told them about the coin and the inner secret of SOUL, about what was inscribed on both sides of the coin, how the coin looked, and how, once received, it had to be given away. How the *coin* was not about *coin*cidence, but about spiritual development; about the adventure of becoming; about the tight connection between what they did and who they were; about the need to stay awake; about how none of this was written down, so it always has to be remembered; about how tough that was; about how easily attention was lost; and about how committed she was to remind them and herself of what was going on.

When she stopped, she saw only stunned faces. Even the seniors, who had heard it all before, were glued. They had never heard it that way. It was like hearing it from someone who had invented it.

Of course Alvin's hand was waving like a windmill.

Ms. A nodded his way and then wished she hadn't.

"How much are the coins worth?" he asked.

CHAPTER 11

THE FIRST SOULS

"Do any other freshmen have questions?" Ms. A laughed as the rest of the SOULs groaned.

"Where are the sophomores?" asked Kate DiGiacomo. Then she turned to Alvin and quietly whispered, "I heard that there were cute sophomore guys in this group."

"They didn't get invited back this year," said a student in the back.

"*Invited Back*??? What's up with that?" Kate replied, spinning the charm on her necklace.

"You can come in on your own as a ninth grader, but you have to be invited back as a sophomore," Dana explained.

"So you can get kicked out?"

"You can *not* be invited back."

"What did they do to get kicked out?" Kate asked.

"They didn't do anything."

"Then why weren't they invited back?"

"Because they didn't *do* anything."

Ms. A raised her hand. The group went silent.

"Enough questions for now. Anyone want to see what the founders of SOUL looked like?" she asked, holding up her mother's copy of the 1971 Kennedy High yearbook.

"Yeah!!!" everyone said with excitement.

Everyone perked up in their seats, eager to get a look.

Ms. Allister carefully opened it to the senior pages and held it up for everyone to see—like a second-grade teacher reading a story to her students. Everyone leaned forward in their desks.

"Here's Tony Happold."

"Look at that afro!!!" someone said with amazement. Everyone smiled.

"I'm jealous!" Derrick Lamay said.

"Where is he now, Ms. A?" asked junior Angela Muñoz.

"Went to Vietnam and never came back."

Everyone stared silently. Then Derrick read the caption under Tony's picture out loud:

Tony Happold AKA "Stick." Loves baseball and driving his four-on-the-floor. Favorite group: The Temptations. Dream: Play ball in college. Favorite Memory: The concert, junior year. Pet Peeve: Having to name a pet peeve.

"Here's Alexander Lucan," said Ms. A, slowly turning to another page she had marked with a yellow sticky note.

"Whaaaaat ???" exclaimed junior Scott Belkat. "Look at those glasses!!!"

"I thought he'd be cute," Dana said, "or strong . . . or something."

"I thought he would have long hair," said Ben Alvarez.

"Weren't they all hippies?" he asked.

"Being a hippie wasn't about long hair, or wearing tie dye, or being really laid back. My mother says being a hippie was all about the way you were inside your head," Ms. A explained.

"Your mother?" asked Ellen Linh.

"This is her yearbook. She was a sophomore then. She was in the first SOUL."

"No way!" said Ben.

"Cool!" said Dana.

Scott Belkat read the caption under Alexander's picture for everyone else to hear:

Started the Save Our Urban Life club. Favorite group: Neil Diamond. Dream: To see the soul. Favorite Memory: The Library Puzzle. Pet Peeve: People who aren't thinking.

"Where is he now, Ms. A?" asked Ellen.

"Nobody knows. His family moved to California after he graduated."

"We should look him up on the Internet!" Robbie blurted out.

Everyone else turned and looked at him. No one said a word. Robbie couldn't tell if he had made a good suggestion or not.

"And here's Elise Waters," Ms. Allister continued, flipping to another tagged page.

"There's your hippie chick!" chuckled Scott.

Everyone laughed. Elise Waters looked like the perfect flower child.

"LOOK AT HER!!" marveled Angela.

She had long, straight brown hair, big innocent eyes, a sweet smile, and a real flower tucked next to her right ear.

Dana read aloud the writing under Elise's picture:

AKA "Ellie." Loves poetry and good music. Favorite group: Dylan and Baez. Dream: Get in the Peace Corps. Favorite Memory: Kissing T. K. Pet Peeve: Missing Woodstock.

"Who's T. K.?" Dana asked.

Ms. A shrugged.

"Who are Dylan and Baez?" someone else asked.

"Where is she, Ms. A?" asked another.

"Actually, she did join the Peace Corps after college. Taught children how to read in Somalia. Some say she is still there, but nobody knows for sure."

"Hippie chick fulfills her dream," said Scott.

"You go, girl," Ellen Linh said softly to Elise's picture.

Ms. Allister closed the yearbook and turned to Dana. "What's our second project this year?"

"Oh, yeah. The second thing we have to do this year is revise our website. This summer I took some time to skim all of the SOUL sites. There are hundreds of SOUL groups across the nation. Most of the other schools have completely updated their sites. And we haven't! That's just unacceptable considering Kennedy High started it all. From what I understand, our site was created four years ago by some seniors. No one has touched it since then. I didn't give it any attention last year at all. So we *really* need to make revising the 'SOUL of The K' website one of our top priorities. We need to clean up the design, update all of the content, stuff like that. And, I want to make sure that we link to all the other SOUL groups. Plus, we need to reclaim the fact that it all started here," answered Dana.

The juniors and seniors all slumped in their seats. SATs, and ACTs were the only extra things they had time for. No one wanted to touch this one. Revising a website took time.

"I'LL DO IT!!!" Robbie Matthews didn't realize he had shouted. But he couldn't help it. Computer stuff was one of his top three things.

Dana Calli looked to see if anyone else wanted to do it or objected to Robbie's doing it. No one moved.

"Okay. Great. Thanks!" she smiled.

"Ms. A, can I borrow that yearbook so I can scan the pictures of the founders? That way I can post them on our site," Robbie asked.

"Sure, but give it back to me by Friday," she said.

Then turning to the group she said, "Okay, that's it for today. Lincoln Park Zoo a week from this Saturday. We meet at the bus stop in front of school at nine o'clock."

"Aren't we going to ride a school bus to the zoo?" It was Alvin again.

This time, Ms. A decided to answer Alvin. "One of the group's unwritten traditions, is to always take advantage of the existing urban resources."

Alvin once again looked like he didn't get it, but he started writing it down anyway. Ben Alvarez passed Alvin's desk on the way out and whispered a translation, "We take buses and trains."

Alvin's hand shot up in the air again, but it was too late. Everyone was out the door.

"That's a little weird," Alvin muttered to Robbie as he stayed put in his desk.

"What is?"

"How come nobody knows where the founders are?" Alvin wondered as he wrote one last thing in his notebook.

CHAPTER 12

THE WEBSITE

"Can I help you, young man?" asked an old woman with bright red hair. Her hair was tied up in a bun, with bobby pins sticking out. She was obviously one of the librarians.

Robbie was staring at the half-finished puzzle on the massive oak table standing just inside the library's entrance.

"Um . . . yes. We have a sub in History today, and she gave me permission to come to the library to work on the computer," Robbie handed her his pass.

"Well, young man, that's fine, but no horseplay," she raised one eyebrow, looking him square in the eyes.

Robbie looked down at the pass in his hand, thinking, *Horseplay? Who uses that word any more? I haven't heard that since like the third grade.*

As if she could read his mind, the red-haired old lady obliged him, "And don't even think about browsing the Internet, young man. Some freshmen boys came in here last year, and thought they could look at inappropriate sites, spend time in those—what do you call them—oh yes, chat rooms! All kinds of horseplay."

"I won't," Robbie assured her, "But where are they?"

"They're sophomores now," she said.

"No, ma'am, I mean the computers."

"In the back," she pointed.

Robbie found an open computer and dropped his books on the desk. Much louder than he had intended. Several juniors and seniors looked up from their work. He pretended that he didn't see them, quickly turning on the computer.

From the moment he had been assigned as SOUL's new webmaster, Robbie had spent every spare moment he had working on the site. For the last two nights he'd been up past midnight, getting it to look good and making it work better. After 10:30 p.m., when his dad kept telling him he needed to turn off the lights, he kept promising he'd be only another few minutes. Even after his dad was snoring down the hall, fast asleep, he worked. He wasn't sure if the seniors who created the site a few years ago didn't know how to use webpage tools, or whether they didn't have the time to really build it right. But Robbie now had the "SOUL of The K" website refreshed and linked to a bunch of the other schools.

Since there were 1,285 high schools with SOUL across the country, Robbie was going to remind all of them that Kennedy High was where it had all started. He was going to introduce the SOULs across the country to the legendary founders—the famous three who had started the whole thing. He took out Ms. Allister's mother's 1971 yearbook.

Suddenly the librarian was beside him. "Find everything

okay?"

"Yes, ma'am."

"You need an access code to get online. I'll write it down." She held a small piece of paper and was fumbling through her pockets.

"Where's my pencil?' she muttered, still searching her pockets.

"So what are you working on, young man?" she asked.

"I'm in charge of the website for SOUL. I'm the new webmaster," Robbie said with pride in his voice.

"Where's my pencil?" she repeated.

"I see it," Robbie said.

"Where?"

Robbie said nothing. He just looked up at her red hair where an eraser end stuck out of her bun.

She smiled. Her hand rummaged through her hair and returned with the pencil.

"Very nicely done," she told him.

She searched his eyes for a moment, as though she was hoping to find something. She wrote out the code and headed for the front desk.

Robbie went to work, adding a few finishing touches to some of the text he had been working on the last two nights:

Kennedy High

THE BIRTHPLACE OF SOUL

Today there are 1,285 high school SOULs in the United States.

But it all started right here with the SOUL of The K.

Click here for the story.

Then the next screen:

It was 1971. High school seniors were being drafted into the Army. The Vietnam War was out of control. President John F. Kennedy and his brother, Senator Robert Kennedy, had both been killed. Martin Luther King, Jr., had been killed. So had Malcolm X. Protests and demonstrations were happening every where. Lyndon B. Johnson was President. Civil rights became law.

There was also the War on Poverty. The hippie movement ruled. So did Elvis and the Beatles. Someone walked on the moon. The United States and the U.S.S.R. aimed nuclear weapons at each other.

Three seniors at Kennedy High (The K), a new high school in Chicago, Illinois, started their own after-school club to raise questions and think about important issues not being talked about by the media. They wanted to start a club for thinkers and doers, both. They wrote just one sentence to describe their club: "We seek to serve urban life, not only the human, but plants, animals, the earth, and anything else living in or beyond the mysterious universe."

Click here to see them.

Robbie wanted to mention how the first SOUL had also created the Coin, but he wasn't sure about it—Ms. Allister said it had never been written down.

To finish the third webpage, he opened the old yearbook and scanned in the photos of the three founders. He formatted the text box, so that he could type in the yearbook captions under each of the founder's photos.

On the final screen he typed into the text box:

This year the SOUL of The K has agreed to partner with the mayor of Chicago in the City Beautiful Campaign, by taking on the responsibility of keeping the Lincoln Park tunnels and the zoo in good shape. Ms. Jamie Allister is our moderator. Her mother was a sophomore member of the first SOUL. (The pictures of the founders are from her yearbook.) We'll use this site to keep you updated on our work this year. Feel free to click below if you want to stay in touch with us. After all, we are the birthplace of SOUL.

Click here to contact us.

Robbie smiled and said out loud, "DONE!"

CHAPTER 13

MSFITS

"Your time is up," said the voice from over his left shoulder.

It was the librarian again. His forty minute limit on the computer had flown by.

"Did you finish your work?" she asked, peering at the computer screen.

"No. Well almost," said Robbie. "But it's set up, so that I can work on it at home, too."

"Work on what?"

Robbie repeated what he had explained to her earlier. "The website. I'm the new webmaster for SOUL and I have to maintain the site."

"You have poor sight?" she asked, straining to hear.

"No. . . I have to maintain *A WEBSITE* for our after-school club," he said slowly and a bit louder.

"Which club?"

"Save Our Urban Life."

"You're in SOUL?" she asked, finally piecing it all together.

"Joined a few days ago," he nodded, gathering his stuff.

"Good for you, young man. I was the librarian here when they first started it."

"You were? Back in 1971?"

"No need to mention the year, young man."

It was time for introductions.

"I'm Mrs. Fitzsimmons, the librarian."

Robbie's eyes widened. This was "Msfits." Even though he had been at The K for only a few weeks, he had already heard about her. Everyone had.

"I see by the look on your face you've heard my nickname."

"I'm Robbie Matthews." He wasn't about to comment. Instead, he put his backpack down and grabbed the old yearbook. He showed Msfits the cover with the year on it and then opened up to show her the founders.

"Here's Tony Happold," he said opening to the first page, tabbed by Ms. Allister's sticky note. He waited for Msfits to read what it said under his picture.

Turning the pages, Robbie pointed out the other founders. "Here's Alexander Lucan . . . and here's Ellie Waters. They started the club, right?"

The old woman smiled to herself and nodded several times. Then she turned the page back to Alexander Lucan to read more carefully the caption under his picture. Her smile grew wider as she turned to head back towards the front desk.

"Would it be okay if I interviewed you, one day for the website?" he asked as they walked to the front desk.

Mrs. Fitzsimmons didn't respond. She either didn't hear it or wasn't interested. She was still smiling about the yearbook.

"I forgot how much he got from it, how much we both got from it."

"Who? From what?" asked Robbie, now the confused one.

Mrs. Fitzsimmons pointed her chin toward the end of the front desk, where two students were standing, studying something on a table.

"The puzzle. It was Alexander Lucan who gave me that crazy nickname of mine. I'm a puzzle freak. That's why we always have one at the entrance of the library. As it turned out, he was a puzzle freak, too, but with a twist. It was always the pieces that didn't fit that interested *him*—the misfits. He said they were clues to something larger."

Robbie was not sure what she was saying. Was she saying she liked her nickname? But he had another question.

"Mrs. Fitzsimmons," Robbie said, "do they keep in touch?"

"Do you think that just because you don't see people they're not here?"

Robbie was caught off guard. Before he could stop his thoughts, his mother's face came flooding into his mind. He felt both touched and confused, on the verge of something deep and true.

He looked up at Mrs. Fitzsimmons. She was standing there, waiting, like she had all the time in the world.

"Well?" she asked in a voice so welcoming Robbie could not resist it.

"I'm not sure . . . could be . . . maybe," he said.

She put her hand on his shoulder and said, "I like your type of mind, Robbie Matthews. Walk me to the front."

Robbie fell in step with the librarian.

"What type of mind is that, Mrs. Fitzsimmons?"

"Open."

CHAPTER 14

DETOUR

"Everyone here?" asked Jamie Allister.

"Everybody who's anybody," a junior called out.

"What about the freshmen?"

"Nine signed up. Three came to the meeting. Two more will show up after fall sports are over," replied senior Dana Calli.

Ms. Allister was trying to gather the SOULs for their work project at the Lincoln Park Zoo. It was a hot September Saturday, hot enough for everyone to be in shorts and t-shirts. Ben Alvarez and Dana Calli were helping her take attendance.

"I'm not ruining my new shirt today with something disgusting, like leopard dung or some nasty zoo stuff," Kate thought to herself, as she and the others boarded city bus #12 to Lincoln Park.

She stared out the bus window and studied the city scenes on the way: people in pajamas, robes, and sweats, reading the morning paper on the steps outside their apartment buildings; sweaty joggers in their running shorts and sports bras; 70-year-old men from the old country dressed in shirts, ties, and 20-

year-old sports coats—hunched over chessboards and checkerboards; elderly women returning from the grocery store with just one bag—enough food for the weekend meals; young girls singing in unison as they jumped rope together; drunks slumped in various alleys, sleeping through their stupors; and beggars standing at the traffic lights, hoping motorists would drop them some change, while waiting for the red light to turn green.

"Morning, Kate," said a boy's voice from the seat next to her.

She was hoping it might be one of the juniors or seniors. For the last couple of weeks, she had been secretly wishing that one of them would ask her to the homecoming dance. She dreamed about wearing something glamorous—having everyone notice how good she looked. Plus, there probably wouldn't be many freshmen girls going with upperclassmen. She'd stand out.

"Hey, Alvin," Kate said flatly.

"So many different kinds of people, huh?" he said. She just nodded and kept looking out the window, away from Alvin.

"And they all seem to accept one another, even though they are all interested in different kinds of things," he continued.

Kate kept silent. Alvin was right—and observant—but she didn't want to talk to him, at least not now in front of everyone on the bus.

"See ya later," Alvin said as he moved back to his own seat.

"Okay!" she said cheerfully, faking it.

She kept looking out the window and twirling strands of her hair around with her fingers. The bus was moving past the boutiques on the Near North. Kate watched stylishly dressed women move from one shop to the next. She noticed the expensive sunglasses they wore, even though it was only nine in the morning. She noticed their beautiful haircuts.

She noticed the way the guys looked like they had stepped right out of the ads in all her magazines. She stared at the cozy couples with their arms around each other, as they strolled down the sidewalk or sat and sipped lattes together. They seemed confident and carefree. Kate daydreamed she was one of them, dressed in fine clothes and jewelry. Feeling beautiful. Being so definitely beautiful.

In her day dreamy state, she barely heard Ms. Allister announce, "Next stop."

And she hardly noticed all the kids picking up their backpacks. But when the bus came to a complete stop, she realized everyone was pushing down the aisle to get off.

Her beautifully dressed day dream came to an end.

She jumped to her feet and got to the door, just as it was closing. But she had forgotten her backpack.

"Wait!" she said to the bus driver.

The bus driver waited, tapping her fingers on the steering wheel, as Kate hurried to wrestle her backpack from under her seat and get off the bus.

Kate smoothed out her clothes, fixed her hair, and took a breath. The rest of the kids were already a half a block ahead, and beginning to turn right at the corner.

They don't even know I'm not with them, she thought.

At first she was disappointed that no one knew she was missing, but that feeling left her as fast as it had come. Another thought took its place. Kate obeyed it.

Automatically.

CHAPTER 15

BUYING BEAUTY

They don't know that I'm missing. I can skip out and make a run through the shops. I'll catch up later, Kate thought to herself.

The boutiques that she was dying to visit were only two blocks back, and on the same street.

It'll be easy, she thought.

It *was* easy.

The sale sign in Angela's Jewelry Boutique was as big as the entire window.

"What's the sale price of that silver necklace?" Kate asked a woman behind the counter.

"Thirty-six dollars plus tax," smiled the woman, taking the necklace out of the display case.

Kate's eyes widened. "That's it? Thirty-six dollars!!"

"It *was* $120. Then it went on sale at fifty percent off, and today you take an additional forty percent off that. It's our one-day Fall Shop-'Til-You-Drop sale."

Kate tried on the necklace, and admired herself in a nearby

mirror. It was perfect. She'd never had a $120 necklace before. She knew that she had $88 in her wallet, the rest of her summer babysitting money.

"Let's do it."

The woman placed the necklace in its box and then in a neat miniature shopping bag, about the size of Kate's hand. Kate put it in her backpack and crossed the street to another shop.

"Such a deal," she told herself. "Fifty percent off, plus another forty percent off today. Today is totally my lucky day!"

She stopped in the middle of the street and went back into the same store, to the same woman.

"Same for earrings?"

"Yep."

Kate found two pairs of earrings, a silver pair and a gold pair, each for $75. Kate looked at the woman, who read the question in Kate's eyes.

"Fifty percent off of $75 is $37.50. Forty percent off of that is $22.50—$23.85 with tax."

But Kate was doing all of the math—about $48 for both pairs. She had about $50 left in her wallet.

"I'll take them," she said.

"Both?" asked the woman.

"Yep. Uh, wait. Let's just make it the gold ones."

Kate figured that she already had a new silver necklace. Gold earrings would be something different. Plus, she wanted to keep some money for the movies and stuff on weekends. At least until she could do some more babysitting.

Once again the woman placed the jewelry in a small box and put the box in another one of those cute, miniature shopping bags.

Only in this kind of store, thought Kate.

As she was placing the earrings in her backpack, her cell phone rang.

"Where are you?" a male voice asked firmly.

Kate knew she was busted. She figured it was one of the seniors.

"I couldn't get off the bus in time, and I'm trying to get back to the zoo. I'm kinda lost."

"Ms. A is at the Information Center. Get there. Go into the zoo through the North Tunnel."

Kate's heart was pounding. She was scared and embarrassed, and she had lied.

"I'll get kicked out before I ever get in," she thought.

She headed back toward the zoo.

She didn't walk fast—she ran.

CHAPTER 16

PEACOCKS

"What is *this*?" Kate said out loud.

She had run all the way to Lincoln Park. The fall morning air was burning the back of her throat. She had sprinted five blocks, quickly walked one, and then jogged two. Now she was standing inside the Spiritual Heritage Tunnel, just inside the entrance to the park, trying to catch her breath.

The images on the tunnel walls slowed her to a walk. She looked from side to side. She had never seen anything like this . . . *ever*! Then at the far end of the tunnel, she saw a woman with two small children.

"Excuse me," Kate said as she approached them. "Do you know where the Information Center is?"

But the woman's attention was on the two little girls, who were pointing at a spot rather high up on the wall.

"Grandma, look at the pretty chickens," said the older girl.

"They're turkeys," said the younger one.

"They're peacocks and peahens," said the grandmother.

Then she turned to Kate who was studying the various peacocks and peahens that were the focus of the mural. At the front stood two peacocks. Behind them, the others were less visible, and even a little blurry.

"I'm sorry," the grandmother said. "What did you ask?"

"The Information Center?"

"Oh. When you leave the tunnel, take the path. If you pay attention, you will see signs."

Kate was on her way when the grandmother stopped her.

"Could you do me a favor? I want to show the girls, but they're too small to get a good look. I can't lift them both at once. Could you lift one for me?"

Kate wanted to say she was in too much of a hurry, but somehow she couldn't say no.

She picked up the smaller girl, perhaps three years old. The grandmother hoisted the older one, who was about four.

"See the two peacocks there at the front?" the grandmother said, pointing. "One *without* its beautiful tail fanned out, and one *with* its beautiful tail fanned out."

"IT'S BEAUTEEEFULL, Grandma!!!!" said the girl in Kate's arms.

"Which one?" asked the grandmother.

"The second one!" exclaimed the four-year-old, "the one with the pretty feathers."

"The first one is just as beautiful," the grandmother instructed. "Only he has decided to hide his beautiful feathers for today. His feathers have all the beautiful colors of the second one, except that he hasn't opened them up."

"Are you sure?" asked the four year old.

The grandmother turned to Kate. "Isn't it true that the plain peacock has just as much beauty as the colorful one?"

The little girls looked at Kate, waiting.

"I never thought of it that way. But yes, the first one has just as much beauty as the second one," Kate paused. "But they're peacocks. Both boys, right?"

"They are," answered the grandmother. Then, looking at her granddaughters and tapping both on the head, she made her point, "But the same thing goes for girls."

Then she looked at Kate. There was fun in her eyes.

"Should we add pretty-colored paint to the first one's feathers to make it more beautiful?" asked the grandmother, enlisting Kate as a teacher's helper.

"Not at all. Why put extra things on the first one when it already has all the beauty it needs?" added Kate.

"Girls," the grandmother said, and somehow Kate felt included, "all beauty begins by hiding on the inside and then slowly coming outside, where it can be seen. You can't go the other way around. Something on the outside can never make the inside beautiful."

She said it in a matter-of-fact way, as if it was something everyone already knew.

Kate was stunned. She felt like the grandmother's eyes had seen right into her heart. Maybe it was the way the woman's voice sounded, so sure and peaceful. Or maybe it was the way she only looked half there, because of the shadowy light in the tunnel.

Kate put the child down on the ground, and was about to ask for directions to the Information Center again.

But before she opened her mouth, the woman pointed to the other opening of the tunnel and said calmly, "This is the Spiritual Heritage Tunnel. Go through all of it."

Still pointing toward the light, she said, "There are signs."

Coming out of the tunnel, Kate was temporarily blinded by the bright sun. She squinted to see the signs and began to cross the Lagoon Bridge, while preoccupied with what the woman had said about beauty. The two peacocks seemed to carry a message.

It was the message Kate was pondering when she stopped on the bridge. She needed to sort out what had just happened. She needed to think. She turned around, rested her backpack on the ledge of the bridge, and slipped out of the shoulder straps. She sat down on the bridge and replayed the morning's events in her mind. When she got up, her mind was on the verge of something. She turned abruptly, and her elbow hit the backpack. It tumbled over the edge of the bridge. Kate lunged for it and missed. She watched it fall, hit the green-brown water of the lagoon, and begin to sink. Then she heard herself yelling, "My stuff! Oh no! My stuff!!!"

CHAPTER 17

A LIGHT HOUSE WITH THEIR EYES

"What did you say your name was?" asked senior Ben Alvarez.

"Robbie."

"Okay, Robbie. You'll need these gloves," Ben said. "Put all the trash in this plastic bag."

Robbie's assignment was to pick up paper along the fence line.

"Good, no heavy lifting," Robbie joked to himself.

"It should take you about two hours to do it well. That should put you back here about 11 o'clock," continued senior Dana Calli. "That includes the tunnel."

Robbie nodded.

Ms. Allister broke into the conversation.

Turning to Carl Howard, the administrative assistant to Councilwoman Gray, she asked, "What tunnel is that?"

Martha Gray had sent Carl to keep an eye on things and to

help keep the kids organized. Her exact instructions were that "if anything strange happens—anything at all—call my cell."

"Spiritual Heritage," Carl said. His voice was flat, matter-of-fact.

"No mess, no stress," Robbie whispered softly to himself with a smile.

The section of the fence that separated the park from the neighborhood streets and apartment building, was made of heavy-duty black wire that was eight feet high. It caught street trash—beer cans, liquor bottles, cigars—and all kinds of personal hygiene items—toothbrushes, hair picks, socks, underwear. All different types of nasty stuff.

Within the borders of the park, the fence changed from wire to wood, and from eight feet high to three feet high. Most of the time the small fence was used to keep children from roaming into the woods, or into the equipment and supply areas. Robbie could step over this section of the fence and pick up trash on both sides when he needed to.

After about a half hour of work, Robbie decided to catch up on the sleep he had missed—by getting up so early that morning. There was not another SOUL in sight, so he sat on a bench and dozed off for a power nap. He had dozed off for about five minutes when a voice woke him up.

"The bench is softer than most people think."

Robbie opened his eyes and saw an older man standing over him.

"I take my naps on this bench every once in while, too."

The man was overdressed for a hot September Saturday. He wore an overcoat, which was open, showing a buttoned-up sweater beneath it. Robbie was not sure, but he thought this was a homeless man. At the sound of the man's voice, Robbie jumped to his feet and got back to work.

The man watched as Robbie began to pick up trash near the entrance to the tunnel.

"Wait 'til you go in there. It's quite a sight. Some people think it's weird."

Robbie turned around. The man was looking directly at him and pointing to the tunnel.

"Spiritual Heritage Tunnel. Have a gander."

Robbie was not sure what *gander* meant, but he went into the tunnel.

"Awesome," he said out loud. He couldn't believe all the different symbols and animals. He knew it was full of spiritual meaning. He didn't think it was weird at all.

Robbie didn't have words for what he was experiencing, but he knew he was in another world. He moved slowly from image to image. "This is neat," he said to himself. Then he noticed the brown earth beneath his feet, and the reddish waves splashing along the bottom of the walls. "I'm walking through the Red Sea," he laughed.

Then something caught his attention. A magnet was pulling him, and he followed its draw until he stood before the giraffe. It was running. The wind blew back its small mane along the full length of its neck. There were mountains in the background.

Robbie couldn't take his eyes off the giraffe. He had no idea how long he had stood there.

When Robbie came out of the tunnel, the man on the bench was still there.

"What do you think?" the man asked, taking off his headphones.

"Wild!" Robbie answered.

"Which image did you like best?"

"The giraffe."

The man laughed, "No mystery there. You look like a giraffe, with a shorter neck." The man laughed again, at his own joke.

Immediately, Robbie felt embarrassed. He slumped a little, trying to shrink his gangling body.

"Don't be embarrassed. It's cool. Giraffes are amazing creatures. They're graceful and fast. They were given to kings as gifts. You know why?"

"No clue."

"Take a seat and I'll tell you."

Robbie took off his jacket. He had worn it on the bus earlier that morning, but the day was really warming up. He didn't know what to make of this man, but he was curious. Nevertheless, he decided to stand.

"Be open," he thought to himself, "like Msfits said."

The man closed his eyes and recited a poem from memory.

"The City of Giraffes—a people,
who live between earth and skies,
each in his or her lone religious steeple,

keeping a lighthouse with their eyes."

The man opened his eyes.

"That poem tells you why giraffes were given to kings. Giraffes are the tallest of the animals, and so they see more. They're farsighted. They can see the mountains. They take everything into account. Their eyes are like a lighthouse, making sure people don't crash on rocks and sink to their destruction, when the weather gets rough. Because kings are leaders of people, they need these qualities. They gotta be able to think ahead. See down the road a ways. Figure out how the decisions today will affect them in the future. Know the consequences of their actions. You tracking me?"

Robbie sat up straight, stretched his long neck, and looked off into the distance. He was thinking back to Uncle Shaun's lecture. He had said the same thing.

"Look at me," said the man.

Robbie turned.

"Maybe giraffes are not just for kings," he said.

"Maybe they're for everybody," said Robbie.

The man's eyes were riveting.

"Maybe you need the gift of a giraffe," he said.

Suddenly, there was noise coming from the bridge area. Someone was yelling. Robbie stood up, stretched his neck, and thought he saw Kate.

He ran toward her.

CHAPTER 18

JUMPING WITHOUT THINKING

"My jewelry!!!" Kate shouted. "My jewelry!!!" she shouted again, distress in her voice.

"Where did it go under?" Robbie asked.

"Right there." Kate pointed directly beneath the bridge. There was no movement in the greenish brown water.

"My jewelry was in that backpack. I just bought it! What am I going to do?"

They looked at the calm surface. Sunk beneath it was Kate's backpack.

"What should we do?" she repeated.

Robbie was trying to figure it out himself. He could see that the lagoon didn't have a dangerous current.

He looked to see if there were any adults who could help, but he saw none. He looked at the height of the bridge and back down at the water. He tried to estimate how deep the water was, and if he would hit the bottom hard. Best he could tell, the bridge was low enough and the lagoon deep enough that he could jump in feet first—and not hurt himself. Besides, his height would help him keep his head above water, wherever the lagoon was less than six feet deep.

He did all his thinking within seconds.

Then he began to take off his shoes.

"What are you going to do?" Kate asked.

Robbie didn't answer. He climbed over the stone railing of the bridge and jumped. The last word he heard before the water covered his head was a stunned Kate screaming—"ROBBIE!!!"

The water was cold, and deeper than Robbie thought it would be. Beneath the surface Robbie couldn't see a thing.

The thought immediately came to him, "Why did I do this? Nobody can see in this mess. I'll never find the backpack."

Maybe if he went straight down, he'd find it.

Then he got snagged.

The loop on the right leg of his carpenter shorts got caught on what felt like the stump of a fallen tree. When he first felt the tug, it scared him. So he instinctively jerked around to pull it loose, snagging the back of his shirt, too.

He knew he had to take off his shirt. He was trying to pull it over his head, when he realized he was running out of air. His lungs were bursting.

Suddenly he felt his shorts and shirt break free. It was as if someone under the water with him had pulled the tree and branches away.

He pushed his arms downward and rose toward the surface. As he broke the surface, the first thing he heard was Kate screaming his name.

Then another voice yelled to him, "Grab it, kid."

He opened his eyes, and directly in front of him was a hook. The hook was attached to a long pole. The long pole was in the hands of a man in a zoo uniform, who was standing on the bridge leaning over the railing.

Robbie grabbed the hook, and the man dragged him toward the grassy bank at the end of the bridge.

"Are you okay?!?" asked the zoo worker.

"Yes sir, just out of breath. Thank you."

When he climbed onto solid ground, Kate was right there, yelling at him through her angry tears.

"What were you thinking, Robbie?! It was just stupid jewelry. Not worth risking your life for. What were you thinking?!"

Robbie just looked at the ground.

"You kids with the SOUL group from Kennedy?" asked the zoo guy.

"Yeah," said Kate. She sounded defeated.

The zoo guy nodded. "Stay here. I'll get your supervisor." He went toward the Information Center.

Robbie tried to explain.

"I checked it out," he said slowly between the deep breaths he was taking as he recovered. "The water was calm . . . the bridge wasn't high . . . I was hoping for people in boats. . . "

"But you didn't think about what was under the water, Robbie, below the surface. There's always stuff below the surface!" Kate was still upset.

Robbie nodded, still taking deep breaths. "Couldn't find it . . . Got stuck. . ."

"Are you sure you're all right?" Kate asked more calmly.

She held his hand.

Robbie nodded.

Someone brought over a towel. Robbie took it and began to dry himself and his clothes. Someone else asked Robbie if he needed something to eat or drink.

"I can get it. I have some money. Thanks though."

He checked the pockets of his wet shorts for his wallet. It wasn't there.

"Oh, no. Lost my . . ."

Just then Robbie remembered putting his wallet in his jacket, as he picked up trash. Because he was bending over all morning, his wallet felt more comfortable in his deep jacket pocket, than in his shorts. He remembered taking off the jacket when he had met the homeless-looking man.

He hustled from the bridge and back through the tunnel to the bench. He was too tired to run, too worried to just walk. Kate followed close behind him. The jacket was still hanging on the back of the bench. The wallet was there. The man was gone.

"You got it?" asked Kate.

"Still in my jacket," he said.

Robbie and Kate passed through the tunnel again, back toward the bridge. He stopped and took another long look at the giraffe. Kate was staring at the two peacocks, revisiting the conversation she'd had with the grandmother and the two girls. The stuff about beauty somehow seemed to matter.

Exiting the tunnel and back into the light again, Robbie suddenly stopped. It came to him. The old man, the giraffe, his uncle, his dad, and Kate had all told him the same thing: Think ahead.

Kate couldn't figure out why Robbie had stopped walking.

"What's wrong?" she asked.

"Something's going on around here," said Robbie.

CHAPTER 19

ON THE HOOK

"Do you have hot chocolate, by any chance?" asked Robbie.

"Today's your lucky day," the concession man said with a smile and an accent.

"You can say that again." Robbie thought about how he had almost drowned.

"Lucky you, I start selling hot chocolate beginning every September. Would you like one too, Miss?" the man said grinning.

Kate was preoccupied.

"Yeah, she'll have one, too," Robbie said.

"Three dollars and thirteen cents with tax."

Robbie handed over four bucks from his wallet, and waited for the change.

He and Kate sipped their hot chocolate. It was the best hot chocolate that Robbie had ever tasted.

"Did they send you to find me?" Kate asked.

"Who?"

"The seniors!" Kate shook her head. "I'm about to get kicked out of SOUL . . . and it's only the first day!"

"For what?"

"I was slow getting off the bus with everyone else. I saw the shops and decided to take a little detour. Bought some jewelry. My cell phone rang and some guy—one of the seniors, I guess—was like, 'Where are you?' Tells me to hurry back to the park and meet everyone at the Information Center. So I'm just getting here now."

"Great," said Robbie. "You skip out and I almost drown. We'll both be thrown out."

"You think?" Kate asked.

Robbie looked over her shoulder.

"We'll know soon. Here comes Ms. A with that political guy."

Jamie Allister arrived at the concession stand a step ahead of Carl Howard who had been asked by his boss, Councilwoman Martha Gray, to supervise everything.

"Who wants to go first?" Jamie Allister asked in a no-nonsense voice.

Robbie told his story. When he was done, Kate started. She was only halfway through when Carl Howard left, dialing his cell phone. His boss had to be told.

Kate ended with a confession, "That's how it happened, Ms. Allister. Honest!"

"There are holes in your story, Kate. I just came from the group, and no one there knew where you were. No one made a phone call to you."

"Somebody *did*, I promise. Whoever it was knew I had skipped out and told me where to go. He told me to go to the Information Center. He even told me to go in through the North Tunnel."

"Where would this mysterious person get your cell phone number?"

"Didn't we have to put it on a sign-up sheet or something?"

"No."

Jamie Allister felt like a cop grilling suspected criminals. She didn't like the feeling, but she thought it had to be done. She couldn't let things get out of hand the way they had last year.

She turned to Robbie.

"Here are the zoo supervisor's exact words: 'We can't be responsible for this irresponsibility.'"

"It was stupid of me. I made a mistake," he said.

The word *mistake* triggered Jamie's memory about her mother's advice on handling SOULs: blame less, learn more.

"Why did you do it?" Jamie asked.

"I didn't think ahead," Robbie said. "That's the message I keep getting. If you don't think ahead about the decisions you make, then . . ."

Robbie didn't know exactly how to finish what he wanted to say.

"Then what?" asked the teacher.

"Then you never wake up," he blurted out, not exactly sure he had chosen the right words.

The voice of Jamie's mother returned to her again, reminding her of why she should be in Lincoln Park instead of at the hospital. "If you don't work with them, then SOULs will sleep."

Jamie was quiet. Inside, she was balancing her mother's advice with her agenda of getting tough.

Finally, she said, "Neither one of you is off the hook."

"Ms. A, I don't feel off the hook," said Robbie. "I feel more on the hook than ever. There are a lot of things I need to change. I know I have to start thinking ahead, but I can't do it very well. I just jumped into the lake without thinking about the consequences."

Same with the pornography.

"And it's that way with other stuff in my life, too."

Ms. A looked at Robbie. She thought to herself, *Is this what my mother meant by noticing and being awake? Let's see if anyone else is awake.*

"What about you, Kate. Do you feel on the hook?"

"I think I know why I buy so many things." But Kate was too drained to say more.

"Let's find the group," said Ms. Allister.

They started to leave the concession stand and move toward the Information Center.

The concession man who was listening to everything and waiting for an opportunity called out, "Excuse me. There's your change."

Robbie turned, walked backed to the stand, picked up his money, and said, "Thank you."

At the Information Center, the SOULs were all gathered and ready to go home. Ms. A asked immediately, "Who called Kate this morning after she skipped out?"

"I didn't call her," said senior Ben Alvarez.

"Didn't know that she skipped out," said junior Scott Belk-at.

"Well, *somebody* called me," said Kate.

Ben looked at senior Derrick Lamay.

"Don't look at me," shrugged Derrick. "Why would I be dial-ing a freshman?"

"You probably listed your cell number when you applied to get into SOUL," Ms. Allister pointed out. "I probably have it writ-ten down somewhere, but we *didn't* call you, Kate."

Ms. A waited before she continued. "We're all done here for the day. Since you missed most of the morning's work, Kate and Robbie, you can stay to finish up our final cleanup. Then ask the park supervisor what else he needs to have done. Call me on my cell when you are ready to leave, so that I know everything is okay."

And if you want to stay in the club, be here tomorrow after-noon from 1 to 3:30. Ask the supervisor what he wants you to do."

"Come back tomorrow?" Kate blurted out in disbelief.

"Are you okay with that?" Ms. A wasn't playing.

Kate nodded.

"Oh, and make sure to have your parents call me this eve-ning. You need permission for coming back tomorrow," Ms. A added. "Got it?"

Both Kate and Robbie nodded.

"The rest of us are due to catch the bus back to school in ten minutes. So let's head out of the park and get back to the bus stop. We'll meet again Monday after school."

Everyone gathered their stuff and headed out.

Kate felt so alone. She certainly didn't feel like part of SOUL.

"What *is* your cell number, Kate?" asked would-love-to-be-your-friend Alvin, before heading for the bus.

As usual, Kate ignored him. She had something more on her mind.

"Are you gonna throw us out, Ms. Allister?" asked Kate.

Now the second year teacher felt on the hook. She wanted to be tougher than last year, but she couldn't help but hear her mother's words of wisdom.

"Make sure you both get back here tomorrow," she replied.

CHAPTER 20

THE PRICE OF WISDOM

"Hello? This is Kate DiGiacomo. According to my cell phone, I got a call from your phone around 9:30 this morning." Kate had pulled her cell from her pocket, thankful it hadn't drowned. She wanted to solve the getting busted puzzle.

"Look, young lady, I don't know who you are or who called you. But this is a pay phone next to Kennedy High School. I was passing by and heard it ringing."

"That's weird," Kate said, putting the cell phone back in her pocket.

"What?" asked Robbie.

"I just called the number of the person who called and busted me this morning. The person who told me to get back to the park with the rest of the group."

"So?"

"The call came from the pay phone outside the K! How could someone outside the K know I'd skipped out to go shopping?" Kate said.

"That *is* weird," Robbie said.

"And then call me on my cell, which also means he had my cell number?"

"Dunno."

Kate and Robbie spent another hour scraping unwanted paint smudges off the sidewalk in front of the Information Center steps, freshly painted by SOUL. Then they disposed of the paint rags and scraps left behind by the group. They moved the four picnic tables back to where they had been, when the group first arrived. They checked with the park supervisor for anything else that needed to be done.

"That's good for today. What time did your teacher tell you to be back here tomorrow?" he asked.

"One o'clock," they replied.

"Okay. I'm working the afternoon shift, so I'll be here. Come find me here at the station."

When they were finally leaving Lincoln Park, Kate dialed Ms. A to let her know they had finished for the day. She hung up just as they once again passed the concession stand.

"I need a dog," said Robbie. "Want one?"

Kate nodded.

"Two hot dogs and two waters, please."

Kate was back to pondering. "I think you're right, Robbie. Something *is* going on."

"Told you," Robbie said as he pulled two fives from his wallet, and handed them to the hot dog man. "I keep getting the same messages from different sources."

"Like what?" Kate asked.

"Choices today will affect you later. Obsessing over looks and stuff can screw up the way you see people."

"And the way you see yourself!" Kate added.

"Exactly," Robbie agreed.

"Don't forget your change this time," the concession man laughed.

When they got to the bus stop, Kate called her mom on her cell. Her mom didn't pick up, so she left a message.

"Mom, we're running late. Can you pick me up at the K in about forty-five minutes?"

When they got on the bus, Robbie paid for both of them and put more change into his still-wet pants' pocket.

Kate found a seat and slumped into it. Her mood was sinking. She was tired. She felt stupid for skipping out. She felt bad about Robbie jumping into the lagoon for her stuff. She felt guilty that he had stayed late after everyone else had gone home. Not to mention, he had had bought her food and bus fare. Now there was the long ride back to the K, and she wasn't thrilled about having to tell her mom. Her Saturday night was shot, too.

An Asian woman sitting next to Kate noticed her mood.

"Why so sad?" she asked gently.

The woman had a soft, kind face. Kate felt herself easily opening up to this stranger and told her the whole story about the backpack.

The woman nodded patiently. Her hands were wrapped around the handles of a metal shopping cart she was using to carry her groceries home from the store.

Kate stared out the window and watched the people along the street enjoying their Saturday. Then the bus passed the store Kate had visited that morning.

When Kate saw Angela's Boutique, she turned to the woman and said, "The worst part is that I lost $200 worth of jewelry I bought from that store *right there*! A beautiful silver necklace and a set of gold earrings!"

The bus came to a stop and the woman stood up. She slowly gathered herself along with her cart and made her way toward the door. Just before stepping off the bus, she turned back to Kate. In a low but very clear voice, she asked, "Isn't wisdom more precious than silver and gold?"

Kate sat up, suddenly alert. The words jolted her. It was like someone had just shaken her by the shoulders to get her attention. She leaned against the bus window and watched the woman walk down the street.

Robbie sat down in the seat the woman had vacated.

Seeing Kate's head resting against the window, he asked, "Falling asleep?"

Kate shook her head slowly, still watching the woman until she disappeared around the corner.

"Maybe waking up," she said half to herself and half to Robbie.

Then, turning to Robbie, added, "Something is definitely going on here."

CHAPTER 21

SILLY

"What happened to you? You look terrible!" exclaimed Mrs. DiGiacomo, as Kate plopped down in the front seat. As soon as she pulled up to the curb outside the K, Mrs. D took one look at her daughter's pale and sad face, and knew something was going on.

Something big had rocked her daughter's boat.

"What's wrong, Sissy?" asked Eric from the backseat.

"It was horrible."

Kate's voice was weak and trembling. She was so tired, so upset, and so mad that she was about to cry.

She took a deep breath and told them the whole story, from Angela's Boutique, to the peacocks in the tunnel, to the lost backpack, to Robbie's plunge, and to having to go back tomorrow.

"You went *shopping*?!?" asked Mrs. D, reviewing the story from the top.

"Bought a $125 silver necklace and $75 gold earrings," Kate said flatly.

"WHAAATT?!"

"For $61."

"And a kid nearly *drowned*?" asked Mrs. D, moving to the next point.

"Trying to save my stuff," Kate said, nodding once.

"Your jewelry," emphasized her mom.

Kate couldn't respond. She wanted to say "Yes, my stupid jewelry," but she was still embarrassed by the way she had called for help to rescue her precious gold and silver. It hurt too much to speak. She just looked out the side window of the car and tried not to cry.

"What's a peacock?" asked Eric.

Eric's innocent curiosity brought her back.

"There were these birds painted on the wall of this tunnel in the park. Two little girls were trying to figure out what they were. Their grandmother explained that they were peacocks. The kids loved the one with its beautiful feathers all fanned out, but the grandmother explained that the other peacock was beautiful, too. It just hadn't opened up its feathers yet. We talked about how silly it would be to add paint to that peacock, since it already had colorful feathers inside its folded tail."

"We talked?" asked Mrs. D, still putting all the pieces together.

"The grandmother and I were both explaining it to the kids."

"Interesting. You know peacocks are boys."

"Yeah, but the same thing goes for girls."

"What thing?"

"The message or moral."

"What?" Mrs. D was confused.

"The grandmother told *me* like this secret message, or moral-to-the-story kind of thing."

Kate's mother took her eyes off the road and looked at her daughter, waiting. Kate heard her mom's silence.

"Beauty is from the inside and then it shines on the outside," explained Kate. "You can't make beauty from the outside. Plus, it's a mistake to think you don't have natural beauty, and it's also a mistake to try to show it off all the time. Both peacocks—the one with the pretty feathers fanned out and the one with the feathers tucked away—have natural beauty."

Eric reached over from the backseat and gently patted Kate's shoulder.

"Which peacock are you, Sissy?"

When they got back home, the three of them watched a movie together. But Kate thought about Eric's question the whole time.

She couldn't get it out of her head. She knew she was the one who always wanted—always needed—to strut her beauty. And yet she also thought that she had been hiding the beautiful side of her that was on the inside.

During the movie, she kept glancing at Eric. The more she looked at him, the more she saw how sweet he was, how smart he was, and how beautiful he was. She felt bad about being embarrassed over his nerdy appearance. She even wished they were still in the same school together, so she could be a better big sister to him in public.

But most of all, she thought about her attitude toward clothes and jewelry. Was it like putting extra paint on the second peacock?

It had always seemed so important.

Now it seemed silly.

CHAPTER 22

BULL

"What time you guys heading to the gym?" Robbie asked.

"Five thirty to seven o'clock, same as always. We'll have the whole place to ourselves. You good?" asked Carlos.

"I'm good," Robbie replied. But he hadn't even been home more than ten minutes.

All summer long, Robbie had lifted weights at the Y with Carlos Lomine and a few other guys. They were into it big time—three days a week, sometimes more. Now that school had started and they were busy with homework and after-school stuff, they were trying to set a regular routine. They had decided to definitely stick with Saturday nights. It was their favorite time to go. The weight room was always empty. All the adults were gone, out to dinner or to the movies. But Robbie and his friends still had to figure out a couple days during the school week where they could all meet up.

Changing into his sweats, Robbie wasn't all that sure he really was good for the gym that night. The jump in the Lincoln Park Lagoon had shaken him up. He felt tired and weak. Plus, he and Kate had to work at the park again tomorrow. But what Robbie saw in his dresser mirror pushed him past his fatigue.

He was only into lifting for one reason: he was embarrassed about his body. It was like he never saw his face when he looked in the mirror. He only focused on his arms that were too bony, his chest that was too flat, and his legs which were too long and skinny. As far as Robbie was concerned, lifting weights was the way to fix himself. And his body was badly in need of new parts.

Grabbing his shoes from the closet and the container of whey protein off the dresser, Robbie shot down the stairs to the kitchen. He grabbed a slice of leftover pizza from the fridge, took a big bite, and set it on the counter. Then he poured a scoop of the banana crème powder into a glass of whole milk. The guys had said the powder was his ticket to looking *cut*. Lately, Robbie lived off the stuff.

Robbie stirred the drink until all of the powder dissolved. It was a lot like a melted banana milkshake. He drank it fast, just like he did with breakfast and dinner every day. The first half of the glass didn't go down as easy as usual. For a second he thought he was going to get sick . . . about-to-puke sick. Maybe it was just all the physical and emotional chaos of the day.

"Dad, you have to call Ms. Allister. She wants your permission for me to do extra work at Lincoln Park tomorrow. I'm leaving her cell number on the counter," Robbie yelled to his dad sitting on the back deck with the newspaper.

"I'm heading out to the gym in awhile to lift with Carlos and some of the guys. I'm almost out of protein. Can you spare $25?" Twenty-five dollars bought Robbie a jar of forty servings.

When Robbie had first started using the protein powder, he had worried his dad might tell him to stop. But it was harmless. You could buy the stuff in the natural food store. It was perfectly legal. Robbie made sure to call it protein when he mentioned it to Mr. M. Everyone knew protein was good for the body.

"Yeah, sure. Get it out of my wallet," Mr. M yelled back.

Robbie took the money from his dad's wallet, downed the rest of the shake between bites of pizza, and headed for the couch to take a power nap.

Later, as he walked to the Y, Robbie cracked open a protein bar. He could never get enough of the stuff. Everyone knew it was the key to building muscle mass. He thought about what had happened at Lincoln Park, as he devoured it in four quick bites. He thought about what the homeless-looking guy had told him. Robbie knew that what the guy had said was true. The same went for what Uncle Shaun had said. He knew he put too much emphasis on the outside appearance of his body. Between lifting and surfing the net for porn, he wondered if he was becoming obsessed with how a body looked and not who a body was.

He wondered how all this would affect him later.

He passed the nutrition store where he bought the whey protein and the protein bars. He decided to wait to buy the powder on the way home.

Carlos and the others were already lifting by the time Robbie got there. He hit the first stations of his circuit immediately and started his reps. Robbie knew how important it was to pace himself—just like his magazines said. But tonight Robbie pushed himself too hard and too fast. Plus his body was already fatigued from his crazy afternoon swim. Halfway through the workout he started to get lightheaded.

Then he started to feel nauseous.

He could taste the pizza he had eaten for supper. It had tasted better the first time. Then he started tasting the banana crème whey protein shake and the protein bar he had gobbled on his way to the Y.

"Guys, I think I'm going to get sick." As soon as the word *sick* came out of his mouth, so did the vomit. Everywhere!

Robbie puked on the weights, the weight bench, and even the benchpress bar.

"Aw no! Dang, boy!!!" The guys were grossed out. Then silence. A loud silence.

It stank. It stank so bad that it almost made Carlos puke, but he jumped into the bathroom and ran cold water over his face.

Robbie was embarrassed. His life's most embarrassing moment right there, with pizza puke and protein puke all over the weight room at the Y.

Somebody brought him a wet towel, put it on the back of his neck, and pointed him to the bathroom. He washed his mouth out and cooled his face off. He could hear the guys giggling outside as they watched the custodian clean up the puke.

Then Robbie looked into the mirror. Instead of seeing the body parts he desperately wanted to repair, he saw his face. He saw the look of sadness in his eyes. He saw a desperate look. For a second, he saw something in his face that he had never seen before. He caught a glimpse of his shy and tender soul.

He spit out the last bit of puke still in his mouth. He noticed the yellowish protein in the sink as he washed it clean.

"This is bull," he said to himself.

He went back to the weights and apologized to the guys, as he gathered up his stuff.

"No problem, Robbie. Happens to everybody. We're gonna meet here Tuesday. You in?" said Carlos.

"Don't think so," he replied softly as he finished gathering up his stuff, slowly shaking his head. "I'm getting tired of this."

Carlos repeated, "Don't be like that. Nothing to be embarrassed about. Happens to everybody," Carlos repeated.

"It's not about that," said Robbie, still shaking his head as he left.

As Robbie walked home, he passed right by the nutrition store. Back home, Mr. M found Robbie putting the $25 back in his wallet.

"I called to let your teacher know you have my permission to go to Lincoln Park tomorrow. Had to leave a message on her voicemail. . . You look bad. What's up?" Mr. M asked.

"I puked. It's getting to be too much," Robbie said.

"There's nothing wrong with lifting weights, Robbie. Gives you something to feel good about," said Mr. Matthews.

"I know, but it's not about pouring down the protein, profiling in the mirror, obsessing over my skinny self, and making myself sick over it. Been liftin' for the wrong reason, Dad. Trust me."

CHAPTER 23

A BETTER DAY

"You look better today," Mrs. DiGiacomo told Kate, as they left church and headed for Lincoln Park.

"I *feel* better," Kate replied. "Had some time to think."

Kate was in a much better mood. Going to church always gave her a chance to think, to calm down, and to recover from the past week.

Sometimes she would sing along with everyone else in the pews. And sometimes she wouldn't sing at all. Instead, she would close her eyes and pretend everyone was singing to her.

She hated getting up early on her day off. And she hated the hassle of rushing into the car to get there on time, half-dressed and half-awake.

But there was something soothing about it. That's why it always put her in a peaceful mood. Every week, it helped her piece herself back together.

Deep inside, below all the outside stuff, going to church always had a way of reminding Kate of who she was. And *whose* she was.

As Mrs. D pulled up to Lincoln Park she asked, "What time should we pick you up?"

"About 3:30," Kate replied. "Stay away from the water!" her mother teased.

"Watch out for the peacocks!" her brother added.

Kate smiled. She knew they were trying to make her feel better about having to work another day in the park.

Robbie had taken the bus and was waiting for her at the supervisor's station. They met with the supervisor, who gave them their chores. He asked them if they would mind walking over to the picnic area near the lake to clean up any stray trash.

"Stay out of the water, Robbie," Kate joked as they approached the lagoon.

"Funny," he replied.

They came to the concession stand next to the bridge, right in front of where everything had happened the day before.

"My turn," Kate said. "Want something?"

"I'll take a water."

"Two waters, please," she told the concession guy.

"Hello again!" he said with a smile.

"You know, I saw what happened to you yesterday. You both back again to clean more?"

"Punished is more like it," Kate replied.

"I'll pay for my own," Robbie said, declining Kate's free offer.

"Drink the water this time, don't swim in it," the concession man kidded Robbie.

"Funny," Robbie said once again and glanced at Kate.

"So today is better day?" asked the concession guy as he handed them two water bottles.

"Definitely," Robbie replied slowly. "Anything is better than what happened yesterday and last night."

"What happened last night? "Kate asked.

"Went to the Y to lift weights."

"Last night? After nearly drowning?"

"Been going a lot with Carlos Lomine and some other guys. Pumping up all the time, swallowing way too much protein. Pushing myself, because I can't stand how skinny and bony I am." Robbie was surprised at how comfortable he felt sharing all his feelings with Kate.

Kate listened quietly.

"So last night I gulped down protein with pizza, pushed too hard at the Y, and threw up all over everything. I made a decision right then. I had been lifting for the wrong reason: lifting cause I hate the way my body looks. I was not seeing past the surface. Gonna focus on the inside me for a while now."

Kate was struck with the last thing Robbie said. "Did you say the *inside me*?"

It was almost exactly what she had picked up when talking about the two different peacocks yesterday in the tunnel. She glanced over at the tunnel.

"Yup," said Robbie. "Gonna quit focusing on what the body looks like and focus more on who the body is. Know what I'm saying?"

"Are you saying that working out with weights is wrong?" Kate asked Robbie.

"No, I'm just saying that I was lifting for the wrong reason. If people lift to stay healthy or get stronger or to improve their athletic ability, or whatever, fine. But I was lifting because I couldn't stand the way I looked. Plus, I went overboard. And it can shape my attitudes."

"Attitudes about what?"

That's as far as Robbie wanted to go with this conversation. So he summed it up.

"Dunno yet," Robbie mumbled as he chewed his hot dog.

"Anything else?" asked the concession guy.

"That's it," Robbie said.

"There's your change," he said.

For the next forty-five minutes, they moved through the park from trash basket to trash basket. Kate and Robbie really didn't say much to each other. They were both wrapped up in their own thoughts.

They kept emptying all the trash baskets into three huge green bags, which they dragged along until they found the big dumpster.

"Wonder how much more we have to do?" Robbie asked Kate.

Just then, the park supervisor came by on a golf cart. "Hop on. One more chore and you can call it a day."

"You mean we'll finish early?" asked Kate.

"Yup," said the supervisor. "But I saved the best for last."

They rode the cart right into the Lincoln Park Zoo, right up to the empty stalls where some of the animals slept, the ones who didn't sleep in their daytime cages.

"Oh no," said Robbie, as he spotted a shovel and a broom.

"Take off your shoes, and put on these rubber hip boots. One of you sweeps, and the other shovels. Then rinse off the concrete with the hose over there. Rinse off your tools and boots when you're done. Any questions?"

"You mean sweep up all their poop?!" Kate said, truly shocked.

"Sweep or shovel," laughed the supervisor.

"This isn't bull . . . uh, manure . . . by any chance, is it?" Robbie grinned at the coincidence. "I think I'll take back everything I just said about today being a better day than yesterday."

CHAPTER 24

NO COINCIDENCE

"Hey Dad! I'm home," Robbie called out as he walked through his front door. He had gotten a ride home with Kate.

"Got you some wings for supper. They're on the kitchen counter," his dad yelled back.

Robbie went straight to the laundry room and dropped his clothes on top of the wet ones from the day before, which were still in a pile in front of the washer. He grabbed clean ones and headed to the kitchen for the wings.

"How was your weekend at the park?" Mr. M asked, entering the kitchen.

"Good, actually. But, um . . . strange," Robbie answered between bites.

"Why strange?"

"Talked to this old guy I met on a bench about a painting of a giraffe on the wall of this tunnel. Then my friend accidentally dropped her backpack in the lagoon. I jumped in the lagoon to get it, and I got stuck underwater, and . . ."

"YOU WHAT???"

"The loop on my shorts right there," Robbie explained as he nodded to the wet shorts his dad was about to drop into the washing machine, "got stuck on this branch or something under the water . . ."

"Are you crazy?!!" yelled Mr. Matthews. "Geez!!! What were you thinking?"

"I thought I was doing the right thing."

"By jumping into the lagoon to fish something off the bottom?"

"I know, I know. But I checked things out before I went in. First, I looked for people in those paddle boats, but there weren't any. Then, I saw that the lagoon was calm—no currents, no rapids, no nothing. I saw that the bridge wasn't high, so I knew that I wouldn't kill myself by hitting the bottom. Plus, I figured I could always walk toward the bank because of my height and . . ."

"ROBBIE!" yelled his dad, "That's crazy!"

"I know, I know. I didn't think *ahead*."

Robbie felt good saying that. It felt as though he had now come to understand what the homeless-looking man, the giraffe, Kate, his dad, and Uncle Shaun had said. It was as though he and this idea had become friends.

"Exactly!" said his dad, still really upset.

Robbie headed to the basement and the computer. It was time to log SOUL's first outing of the year.

Chicago's Lincoln Park . . . painted steps . . . fall cleanup . . . 17 of us including 3 freshmen (no sophomores!).

Positive comments from park supervisor and those enjoying the park on this beautiful September Saturday . . . cool tunnels recently restored by the city . . . Spiritual Heritage Tunnel is a must-see. All went well . . . good to get the year off to a good start.

Robbie relaxed and surfed the net for awhile. He checked the SOUL of the K's site every once and awhile to see if anyone had posted a message. Dozens of kids were sending comments about the SOULs at their schools and what they were doing for projects this fall.

"A lot of SOULs out there," he thought to himself.

Robbie got an Instant Message from a mysterious sender—someone with a screen name of OS: "Why didn't you mention the importance of seeing ahead?"

"Kate? Is that you?" he instant messaged back.

"And how you got unsnagged under water?" replied OS.

Robbie pushed his seat away from the computer and stood straight up, staring at the screen in disbelief. Kate didn't know anything about how he had gotten unsnagged. How it was almost as if someone or something had helped him.

No one knew. He hadn't told a soul.

"Who *is* this OS?" he wondered.

Just then, his dad called him from upstairs. "Robbie?"

Robbie found his dad doing laundry.

Mr. Matthews had picked up Robbie's pile of clothes, and emptied the pockets of the shorts and the jacket he had worn on the weekend.

"You left some money in your pants and your jacket." Mr. Matthews held his hand open with the accumulated change.

There was a strange coin among the quarters, nickels, pennies, and dimes. It was a bronze-looking coin about the size of a quarter, but thin like a dime. Robbie picked it up and studied it slowly and carefully.

On one side was a figure like an angel with the words *Truth, Beauty, Love* printed around the coin, making a circle around the angel. On the other side of the coin were the letters *S, O, U, and L* across the middle with the words *See, Judge, Act* printed around it in a circle.

"Where did *that* come from?" asked his dad.

CHAPTER 25

DEFINITELY SOMETHING GOING ON

"Package!" yelled Eric, pointing out the car window to the front door of the house, as the DiGiacomos pulled up the driveway.

"I'll get it," said Mrs. D. "It's probably something I ordered last week."

"Who delivers on Sunday evening?" Kate asked aloud.

"CBS!" Eric replied.

"That's UPS!" Kate giggled, swinging her arm around her brother's shoulder, as they walked through the garage door and into the house.

"It's for you, Kate," Mrs. D called out. "Puhleeez not more clothes from the catalogs!!" Mrs. D gave Kate her credit card to shop from her favorite catalogs on occasion, but lately there had been a few too many packages on the doorstep.

"Shopaholic!" shouted Eric, happily repeating his new favorite way to tease his sister.

Kate automatically began to open the box, but something stopped her.

She noticed that the box wasn't taped shut. Also, it had no postage on it at all.

"FOR KATE" was scrawled on it with a blue magic marker.

"Maybe it's from your boyfriend," Eric said. He was more excited than anyone.

It was heavier than most stuff she ordered from catalogs.

Inside the house, she carefully opened it and could not believe what she saw.

It was her backpack.

Still slightly damp.

She backed away from it for a second. It was like seeing someone come back from the dead. She unzipped the backpack, and looked inside it. Everything was still there. Even the jewelry.

When she saw how neatly the two boxes had been wrapped, Kate's mind flashed back to the sales woman who had sold the jewelry to her.

She opened the two wet jewelry boxes. The silver necklace and the gold earrings were beautiful.

"They're gorgeous," her mom said softly, as she leaned over Kate's shoulder.

But to Kate they had lost their luster.

"I'm taking them back."

"You can't take them back. They've been dumped in a lagoon," said Mrs. D.

"I don't care. I don't want them."

All Kate could think of was how Robbie had nearly drowned

over them and how they would probably get her kicked out of SOUL, just when she was getting something out of it. She didn't want to be kicked out. She wanted to be part of it.

She was angry at the jewelry, but really she was angry at herself. She no longer wanted to depend on pretty things for beauty. She wanted to be free. This was her chance.

Her mother moved from behind Kate's shoulder in order to stand directly in front of her daughter.

"Kate, look at me."

She waited for Kate's eyes to meet her own.

"Maybe you can wear them as a reminder."

Mrs. D had seen something on the front side of the backpack that Kate hadn't noticed yet.

She gently lifted Kate's backpack out of the box, held it up, and turned it slowly so Kate could see a note taped to the front of it.

Isn't wisdom more precious than silver and gold?

CHAPTER 26

SOMETHING'S GOING ON HERE

"Uncle Shaun? This is Robbie."

"S'up Robbie?"

Robbie punched the last key on the computer and nodded his head up and down, while still balancing his cell between his ear and his shoulder. He had finished what he had begun.

"Cleaned up my computer," he said.

"Whaddaya' mean?"

"Tossed it."

"Did what?"

"Got rid of all that mess from the internet."

"The porn?"

"Yup. Deleted all of it."

"There you go."

"Met this weird guy in Lincoln Park."

"Was he wacked?"

"No, no. Not like that. But he got me thinking about stuff."

"Like what?"

"Same stuff you were telling me. How messing with porn

now will affect me later in all kinds of ways."

"Some stranger in the park talked to you about porn?!"

"No not at all. He talked about giraffes."

"Say what?"

"He talked about how I need to look ahead. How I'm built for it."

"Built for what?"

"Built to see down the road. To see how stuff you do today will affect how you do things and who you become later. So that's why I dumped the porn. Sorta' the same thing you've been telling me."

Just then, another call was coming in to Robbie's phone.

"Uncle Shaun, I got another call coming in. Gotta let ya go. Okay?"

"Call me," his uncle said. "You hear me? Call me back!"

Robbie caught the incoming call.

"Hello?"

"Robbie? It's Kate!"

"S'matter Kate? You okay?"

"You won't believe what just happened!"

Kate told Robbie how her backpack showed up at her front door. Then she told him about the woman on the bus who asked her, "Isn't wisdom more precious than silver and gold?" The same question that was on the note that came with the backpack.

Robbie listened the whole time and didn't say a word. He still didn't say anything even after Kate was finished. She noticed his long silence. It dawned on her she had been had.

"You did it! Why didn't you tell me??!! First you pretend to nearly drown in the lagoon, scare me half to death, then you hide my backpack . . ."

"Kate."

"Then you overhear the conversation I have with that woman on the stupid bus."

"Kate," Robbie said a little louder.

"Then you drop off the backpack at my house when we are away at church! With a cute little note!!!"

"Kate!"

"That stinks, Robbie! Not funny at all. Why did you *play me*???!!!"

"Kate! I didn't do *any* of that!"

"Quit it!" she yelled.

"For real, Kate."

The tone in Robbie's voice was strange enough to catch Kate's ear—despite her anger. She stopped.

"You didn't?" she asked.

"I swear."

"Don't swear," she said.

"Well, I'm telling you the truth," Robbie quietly insisted. "Now can I tell you what happened to me?"

"Go," said Kate.

Robbie told Kate all about really getting snagged and then getting unsnagged—like someone may have helped him underwater.

Then he told her about the e-mail from this OS person who could not have known about any of this, unless that person had been under water with him.

"Something going on here," said Kate. "We're being watched."

"More than that."

Then Robbie told her about the coin.

"No way. No way. No way!!! Robbie this is HUGE! Remember what they told us about the SOUL coin?"

"Not really. I wasn't paying that much attention."

"Are you kidding me!? Robbie, you can only get a coin from another SOUL! And not that many people get them! SOULs give the coins away only when they see someone doing something positive or spiritual or something. Only SOULs have these coins. The original SOULs at the K invented the coins. Remember Ms. A telling us the story?"

"What did you say?" he asked.

"Only SOULs have these coins. Only SOULs give them away!"

"No" said Robbie. "Who invented the coin?"

"The original SOULs at Kennedy!!!! Robbie this is so cool. No one at the K got a coin last year. That's one of the reasons there are no soph . . ."

Robbie cut her off.

"OS," he said softly like he was talking to himself.

"Whadya' say?" asked Kate.

"Remember the IM I got about my getting unsnagged under

water?" he was still thinking out loud, "It was from OS. Suppose OS stands for Original SOUL?"

"You mean someone from the original group at the K?" she asked

"Yup."

"Like someone from that group is still around?"

"Maybe."

"Wasn't Ms. A's mom in the original group?" asked Kate.

"Yup."

"Cha-ching," Kate said. "Maybe that's what's going on. Ms. A and her mom are up to something."

CHAPTER 27

BEGINNING

"Now for the hard part."

Jamie Allister was sitting on the desk. She had just called The Kennedy High SOULs to order. Everyone was there.

"Doing the work is one thing. Paying attention is another. That's the hard part. When we were at the zoo Saturday, what did you notice? What did you learn?"

Alvin was ready. "There are seventeen monkeys in the Baboon House."

The SOULs groaned.

Ms. A laughed. "We always need an accurate count, Alvin. But try looking a little deeper."

Junior Scott Belkat, piped up, "Not everybody showed up on time."

Kate sunk down into her seat.

"You have an eye for mistakes, Scott."

Ms. A looked around at the group, "How about some more positive observations?"

The group was silent. Nobody was looking up at Ms. A.

Kate looked over at Robbie. Her eyebrows went up.

"I think something might be going on," Robbie mumbled.

"What did you say, Robbie?"

He said louder. "Something might be going on?"

"I hope so," Ms. A laughed. "Otherwise what would we notice? So what do you mean?"

"We're being watched."

"Really?"

"Somebody knew everything that happened at the zoo. Even things I didn't tell anyone about. He knows my email address, and he instant messaged me. He signed it OS."

"Who's OS?"

Robbie looked over at Kate. He wanted her to tell about the backpack. But she looked the other way.

"Who's OS, Robbie?" Ms. A probed.

"We thought it might be your mom."

Ms. A slid off the desk, walked over to Robbie, and sat down in a student desk.

"My mom's in the hospital, Robbie. I'm going to see her right after this meeting. I don't think she had time to be sending you instant messages."

Robbie felt like an idiot. Kate had her eyes closed, like she was praying to become invisible.

"Sorry," Robbie said quietly.

"Why did you think it was my mom?"

"I thought OS meant Original Soul and your mom was in the original group, wasn't she?"

"She was. But why did you think an Original Soul would be sending you an instant message?"

Robbie hesitated. Finally, the words came out his mouth very slowly.

"I . . . got . . . a . . . coin."

He reached into his pocket, took out the coin, and put it on the desktop.

The group exploded. Seniors Ben Alvarez and Derrick Lamay bolted out of their seats to see it. Seniors Ellen Linh and Dana Cali called out, "Is it a SOUL coin?"

"NICE!!!" yelled Ben.

"We haven't seen one in two years!!!" said Derrick.

Robbie was embarrassed.

"I don't even know what the inscription means," he muttered.

Ms. A was about to explain, but Alvin, consulting his notes, beat her to it.

"It means that a former SOUL saw you embrace an experience of Truth, Beauty, or Love. See those words on the one side of the coin?"

Robbie nodded.

Someone said, "Pass it around."

The coin went from hand to hand.

Ms. A took up where Alvin left off.

"Or it means that a SOUL saw you SEE, JUDGE, and ACT in a way that nurtured someone else's spirit. See those three words on the other side of the coin?"

It took a while, but everyone in the group got to look at the coin, both sides.

"That's what I meant," said Robbie. "Something was going on. Somebody had to be at the zoo watching me."

"SOULs are everywhere," Ms. A said, smiling.

The buzz in the room was crazy good. Everyone was pumped. Being a SOUL meant something totally different and totally new to everyone now. Now they knew—or now they remembered—that they were connected to a bigger group. A group of good SOULs who lived out there . . . beyond the K.

"You know," said senior Ben Alvarez as he handed Robbie back the coin, "now that you have a coin you can give it to someone else you see 'doing the do.'

Robbie nodded.

He knew who that was and the time was now. He was about to give the coin to Ms. A. She had patiently listened and tried to understand how he decided to jump in the lake, and had not yelled at him when he was so stupid to think her sick mom was behind it all.

But before he could do that, Ms. A spoke up.

"It's not that simple. First, you have to know why you received the coin. It is in knowing why you received the coin that you will come to understand who to give it to. Getting a coin is not the end. It's a beginning."

Ms. A smiled at Robbie. "Think about it for the next few weeks," she said. "Everything doesn't have to happen at once. Time brings more understanding."

Robbie thought back and realized he didn't know anything. He didn't know how his pants got unsnagged, how the coin got into his pocket, who sent the email, or who the man was that knew so much about giraffes.

But most of all, he had no idea how a coin that was about Truth, Beauty, Love and Seeing, Judging, and Acting for the good of others, could be given to someone who recklessly jumped off a bridge and only recently had the guts to stop a very bad habit or two.

Robbie put the coin in his pocket.

CHAPTER 28

SOULS ARE EVERYWHERE

"Ms. Allister?" asked the caller.

"Yes."

"This is Carl Howard from Martha Gray's office."

The SOUL meeting had ended an hour ago and Jamie pulled into the hospital parking lot. She had gone there right after the SOULs had finished at Lincoln Park on Saturday. Sunday she had spent the afternoon and evening at her mother's bedside. Katherine was recovering from the operation fine, but she was still "out of it," sleeping almost all the time. This afternoon she would be more responsive.

"How are you doing?" Jamie answered Carl.

"Fine. Is everyone all right?" asked Mr. Howard.

"What do you mean?" asked Ms. A, as she got out of her car and walked toward the hospital entrance.

"Well there was that boy who jumped into the lake. And that girl who skipped out. I was wondering if all that worked out ok."

"I just came from a meeting where we began to take care of it, actually."

"Good. After what happened yesterday, Councilwoman Gray had some concerns about whether or not to continue using students as part of the Lincoln Park Project. She was concerned that the city may be held liable if the kids got injured by doing foolish things—like jumping in lagoons," he said.

"I think we're beyond that," Ms. A replied.

"I hope so. The park supervisor had wonderful things to say about your students. He called us first thing this morning. We just are a little concerned. By the way, did any of your students report anything strange regarding the Spiritual Heritage Tunnel?"

"I have no idea. But all our kids are just fine."

"That's great. So let's keep going on schedule. Your group is due back at the park to help out with the children's Halloween festival the last weekend in October," he said.

"Right. I have that information," she said.

"Okay then. We'll see you and your students again in October," Carl said.

Jamie turned off her cell as she entered the hospital, and took the elevator to her mother's room on the third floor.

"Hi Mom!" she said with a smile.

"Hey," her mother weakly smiled back.

"How you feeling?" asked Jamie.

"Good. Groggy but good. I was out of it yesterday. And I'm still a little groggy. The pain medicine really affects me . . . how did the SOUL meeting go after school today?"

"I'm starting to get it," Jamie said.

"Get what?"

"My role with SOUL."

"Is this about getting tougher again?" asked her mother.

"Nope. It's about helping them notice. Everything's always evolving, isn't it?" Jamie asked.

Katherine smiled, "Yes, and that's a good thing to know."

"Guess what," Jamie said, changing the conversation, "one of the kids received a coin. He has no idea why and even I'm a bit puzzled."

"That's always the way. It takes time to know."

"He thought you had something to do with it, Mom."

"SOULs are everywhere," she laughed weakly. "But I've been otherwise occupied."

Katherine's eyes were starting to close when Jamie's dad, John Allister, came in.

"Sorry I'm late. Traffic was a mess. Monday night football. Bears are home tonight against the Dolphins," he said as he took off his jacket and softly kissed his wife's forehead between the eyes.

Katherine smiled and motioned Jamie to come closer.

"Who did you say got a coin? A bear . . . a dolphin . . . or a giraffe?" she whispered as she started to nod off to sleep

Jamie knew nothing about a giraffe. She saw the confused look on her dad's face.

"Maybe the talk of the Bears-Dolphins game confused her," he said.

Jamie was confused too. She shrugged.

"No mom, a ninth grader named Robbie Matthews."

TO BE CONTINUED.

TURN THE PAGE FOR A SNEAK PEEK OF VOLUME 2

"This is the last one," gasped the guy in the pirate mask.

He was out of breath. It was late Halloween Eve, just before midnight, and he and his companions had been running through Lincoln Park from tunnel to tunnel—leaving their messages on the walls.

"I hate to see the fun stop." The gnarled lips of a Frankenstein mask formed the words.

The other two, Mickey Mouse and Superwoman, laughed, but said nothing.

The Halloween tricksters pulled spray paint cans from their pockets. Ten minutes later, when the last of the paint sputtered out, they were breathing heavily, like some strenuous task had taken everything out of them.

Then all four vandals turned their flashlights on the walls. For a moment they were silent, the beams crisscrossing, lighting up the explosion of images.

"What the hell is this?" said the Pirate.

Superwoman, who carried the plans for the Halloween prank, pulled a scrap of paper from her jeans' pocket. The beam from her flashlight moved down the page.

"We've done Great Americans, World of Animals, Children Count, Workers of the World, and Family Life. This must be Spiritual Heritage."

The flashlights went back to their work, exploring the walls.

"Here's a cross," said Mickey Mouse. "But it's got flowers on it. It's not burning."

"There's the Jew star of David," grumbled Frankenstein.

"Here's that pregnant Mexican Mary." Superwoman had spotted her.

"There's a black jerk with his arms out," said Mickey Mouse.

They all turned to the pirate.

"This stuff is exactly what we hate."

Then they stood in the middle of the tunnel and slowly turned, reviewing the damage with their flashlights.

"Alright!" said Frankenstein.

"Better than alright!" said the pirate.

Frankenstein, Superwoman, and Mickey basked in the pirate's praise.

Superwoman knew it was time. She positioned the flashlights, took the camera from her pack, and had the pirate, Frankenstein, and Mickey line up in front of the hate-filled words they had scrawled on the walls.

"Now smile," she said.

It was the sixth time that night she had said that. And for the sixth time they laughed again, safely hiding behind their masks. The picture was proof of their prank.

The night raid was over. They clicked their flashlights off and began walking toward the front of the tunnel that led out of Lincoln Park Zoo. But some instinct made them suddenly run, each step taking them into the largeness of the city where their deeds could not be traced.